"YOU MAY BRING ME NOTHING," HE SAID STERNLY.

"I am able to fetch it myself."

"No, no, no, that would not be Greek," she whirled back to the table and picked up an earthware pitcher. "Here, a good wife waits on her husband." Pouring milk into a mug, she brought it back to him.

Taking it, he smiled. "I certainly did not mean . . ." he paused, staring at her hands—they were reddened and the nails broken. "What have you been doing?"

"Only a little washing. The soap is strong. But it was necessary," she insisted. "We needed clean clothes and furthermore, you will be able to use your wits for purposes more important than making up reasons as to why your 'woman' has 'fine lady hands.'"

He looked down suddenly. Then, because he was unable to restrain himself, he set down the mug of milk carefully and taking her hands, he pressed one and then the other to his lips. . .

Novels by
Zabrina Faire

Lady Blue
The Midnight Match
The Romany Rebel
The Wicked Cousin
Athena's Airs

Published by
WARNER BOOKS

Your Warner Library of Regency Romance

Athena's Airs

Zabrina Faire

WARNER BOOKS

A Warner Communications Company

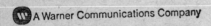

One

Gray clouds were increasing in that area of the sky that stretched over England and particularly over London's Grosvenor Square; the draperies in Lady Caroline's drawing room were being chivied about by a breeze which was showing distinct signs of becoming a wind—not entirely unwelcome in a July that had been uncomfortably hot.

Lady Caroline, with a wary eye to the elements and another to her niece Athena Penrose, sighed. Two storms were brewing and though she regretted both, she preferred the inclement weather outside. One could close one's windows against that—an argument with her spoiled and tempestuous young relative was far less easy to combat, especially since she could not but feel sorry for the child. It was an emotion that made her own rebuttals extremely ineffective at a time when she should have been stern and unyielding.

Though it had been over five months since the debacle that Lady Caroline called "Athena's disappointment" had taken place, the marks of it were still evident in the girl's brooding eyes and in the downward droop of her mouth. Both features bespoke an inward misery that was expressing itself in a distrust of all the other young gentlemen who still pursued her. Lady Caroline had told her niece repeatedly that she was fortunate in discovering the perfidy of her intended before rather than after their marriage, but nothing could convince the child that her heart was not broken beyond mending. Though Lady Caroline could not bring herself to tell her niece that it was her strongly developed sense of pride that had suffered the worst blow, she herself was convinced of it. In fact given Athena's outrageous plan, she was sure of it. Her niece was bound and determined to put as many leagues as possible between herself and a city where her fiancé, the handsome young Marquis of Eames had, only days after he came into his fortune, eloped with an opera dancer!

Lady Caroline, her anxious eyes fixed on Athena's lowering countenance, stifled the sigh that expressed a complicated series of regrets. If only the girl had not been sequestered in the country with her scholarly and indulgent parents for the greater part of her eighteen years—if only those parents had not died within six months of each other—if only Athena had not been left in control of her sizable portion—if only she had listened to her aunt, who had hinted that the Marquis was pursuing her for that same portion, his name having been linked with the said dancer for years (though none of the ton had dreamed he would marry the creature!)—if only he had not come into his own partrimony, thus making it unnecessary to pursue the heiress—*then* Athena would be heart-whole and in possession of those senses which would have enabled her to recognize the folly of embarking upon the journey which she now proposed!

Lady Caroline looked up at her niece and then

sat down quickly. It was usually better to have a standing rather than a sitting argument; but with Athena, either way, she was at a disadvantage. The girl was preposterously tall—fully seven and a half inches over five feet and, though beautiful, her appearance was extremely unfashionable. Lady Caroline had been told that she resembled her Italian grandmother—so unfortunate that Sir William Penrose had wed a foreigner with such marked characteristics! Nearly all of them were represented in Athena—great masses of heavy, blue-black hair, an olive complexion, a full red mouth set in an oval face, a lovely straight nose and, by way of contrast, Lady Caroline's sister Anthea's vivid azure eyes. It was an arresting combination but, coupled with her height and a full-busted figure which was a shade too plump, it was not the thing. Indeed, she could imagine that it might have been most disconcerting for Eames to contemplate marriage with a female bigger and heavier than himself—the opera dancer being the merest wisp of a girl. Lady Caroline sighed a second time. "You cannot consider it, Athena," she said patiently. "It is not at all . . . well, it is not done."

"It will be done," Athena replied coldly. "I shall do it or, rather, we shall. It is a sacred trust."

"One that was left to your brother Ares, *specifically*," Lady Caroline reminded her.

"Would you have wanted Uncle Hobart to have been buried and you not present at his funeral?" Athena demanded.

"That . . . is quite different. And I—I think you are most unkind to remind me of Hobart's demise." Lady Caroline sniffed and, for a brief moment, wished she had not doffed her widow's weeds. She had been glad enough to be rid of them, it was true, never having admired herself in black—so dimming! However, had she been wearing black, she would have been entitled to make play with a black-bordered handkerchief, waved in a hand embellished with the huge onyx mourning ring she had also discarded as soon as custom dictated. As it was, she could only clasp her diamond-bedecked fingers and say, "Furthermore, Sir Hobart did not require me to cremate him and scatter him over a heathen mountain at the other end of the world. He was quite content with the family plot."

"Papa and Mama were passionately addicted to Greece—as witness our names," Athena countered.

"I know," Lady Caroline reminded her. "I know all about it. I have a large bundle of Anthea's letters on that very subject. However, I think that in their zeal of matters classical, your dear parents failed to take into account the country's conditions. Greece is in a state of turmoil, filled with Turks and bandits which, I am sure, are one and the same thing, not to mention the Greeks, whom, I understand, are not above a little banditry themselves and—"

Athena drew herself up to her full height. "I pray you will not disparage that most unfortunate and betrayed people," she intoned. "That the inheritors of the mantle of Aristotle, Socrates, Sophocles, Homer and Euripides, not to mention Pericles, Aristophanes, Aeschylus and Demosthenes, should be forced to suffer under the heel of the Turkish tyrant for five hundred years—with no aid from European nations, who owe their culture, nay, their very existence to the Greek Civilization, passes all comprehension!"

"I daresay," Lady Caroline murmured, "but no

doubt they have their reasons. And I am not about to discuss political history with you. I am only saying that an expedition such as you propose is far too arduous and dangerous for a female to undertake."

"Mama undertook it."

"In company with your Papa, who spoke the language and—"

"Papa taught it to both Ares and myself. In addition, we speak ancient Greek as well."

A third sigh troubled Lady Caroline's diaphragm. Athena's education was another sore point with her; rather than being instructed in the social graces, she had enjoyed much the same schooling as her brother Ares, save that Athena, much to her oft-expressed disappointment, had not been able to accompany Ares to Cambridge. However, she had continued to pursue her studies. To date, she was alarmingly proficient in Greek, Latin, Italian, French, astronomy, mathematics, history and botany. She could also ride, swim and shoot. Her main lacks were in the feminine accomplishments of sewing, embroidery, household management, drawing, painting and the pianoforte; though she did have a lovely voice, which she steadfastly refused to air in drawing rooms after dinner, saying that she hated the sentimental ditties that were the fashion and was not going to sing about forlorn violets to gentlemen who were three parts drunk. Lady Caroline felt it incumbent upon herself to state, "I know you have a fine education, my dear, and no doubt your facility in languages could stand you in good stead. But it is not fitting that a young girl venture into so wild a territory and—"

"You speak as if I were doing my venturing alone. I will be accompanied by Ares."

9

"Who can be amazingly heedless. Think of that scrape last year; it nearly got him sent down from Cambridge."

"That was not his fault—and he did *not* get sent down, which, I think, is proof of that." Athena's eyes flashed.

Lady Caroline could wish she had not criticized that headstrong and stubborn young man—it served no purpose, for Athena believed in him wholeheartedly and sprang to his defense like a tigress. She swallowed an air-bubble of nervousness. "I am loath to remind you of—of your pain. I know you suffered greatly, but though you might not credit it now, it was all for the best and there are other worthy gentlemen who . . ."

"Please, Aunt Caroline." Athena frowned and raised her hand. "I beg you . . ."

"Child," her aunt continued determinedly, "I think it would not be a bad notion to leave London now, just for a change of scene—Bournemouth or Brighton, say. But if you go to Greece, you might be there many months . . . you could miss the whole season. Do not forget, you'll be nineteen in a week! You could be past twenty by the time you return and you ought to be settled."

"*Sold*, I presume you mean," Athena returned bitterly. "Sold to the highest bidder, being careful that this time his fortune matches mine."

"My dear, just because Eames—"

"Aunt Caroline, do you imagine that I regret his decision? As you have said, better now than later. Furthermore, it has opened my eyes. An heiress is very like a horse. She is put on a block and auctioned off like a prize mare at Tattersall's. Then, she is stabled in the country to breed a son and heir while her stallion dallies with his mistresses or his opera dancers or both in town. I think it is very, very fortunate that Eames resolved to wed his opera dancer rather than myself. I assure you I will not be so deluded again. I have resolved never to marry."

"My dearest Athena," gasped her aunt, "you cannot mean it!"

"I do most certainly mean it," Athena retorted. "I am through with love."

"Oh, oh, oh, Athena," Lady Caroline breathed. "I do not know what is to become of you."

"But I have told you what is to become of me, Aunt Caroline . . . for the next few months at least. I am going to Greece with my brother Ares."

It was near five in the morning but in that discreet establishment known as Brooks, the play was as deep as ever. Gathered around the large tables were numerous gentlemen engaged in faro or macao, sipping what might have been their fifth or fifteenth glass of wine, while the director of the club and his hirelings looked as fresh as if the hour were its afternoon equivalent. Moving among the players, servants quietly replaced guttering candles and removed scores of empty bottles, while, at the door, an usher stood ready to light those who had had their fill of gambling to the street.

"I vow, Sir Ares, you'll not be leaving," a gentleman muttered as a tall, fair-haired young man stuffed a thick packet of banknotes into the pocket of his brocade vest.

Sir Ares, raising a golden eyebrow over eyes as dark as his sister Athena's were blue, nodded, a twist of a smile lifting a corner of his mouth. "Fear I must," he said. "I'll come back this evening, perhaps Turnbull."

"But think," Mr. Turnbull said persuasively, "your luck's running high. You might increase two-fold what you've just won."

"This evening," Sir Ares said firmly, his smile broadening as he caught the look of discomfiture in Turnbull's small, flickering eyes and knew him to be a "puff," one who egged the unwary on to reckless and ultimately disastrous play. As he rose from the table, he sighted an acquaintance, Sir Edwin Calthrope, standing by the fireplace watching two gentlemen at cards. Moving to Calthrope, he said, "They must think me a flat." He was about to launch into a lively description of Turnbull's efforts in his direction, when he noted that Sir Edwin was looking very grave. "I vow," he smiled, "why so sour a countenance? You did well enough tonight."

"Of a truth, I did." Sir Edwin stepped away from the table, muttering, "But poor Herriot's had a damnable run of luck. Can't understand it. Piquet's his game . . . came here to repair his fortunes with it, shouldn't be surprised if his pockets are quite to let."

Glancing at the player in question, a lean, dark man in his late twenties, Sir Ares shrugged. "I wish no one ill, of course, but Herriot's an uncommonly unpleasant sort. Spoke to him earlier in the evening. You told me he was back from the Levant. I know he's written books on traveling in far places. Thought he might have some pointers for my sister and myself. As you know, we're off to Greece at the end of this month but, beyond telling me in a very nasty tone of voice that females had no place on such an expedition, he'd not a word to spare for me. Fellow was damned rude."

"You shouldn't have mentioned females," Sir

12

Edwin said sagely. "He dislikes the whole breed of 'em. Not that he doesn't have his reasons. I happen to know a bit about him, comes from the same county. He's difficult, right enough, but for all that he's a man of honor. Shouldn't like to see him languishing in debtor's prison."

"Good God, is there a chance of that?" Sir Ares questioned.

Sir Edwin nodded. "He's been staying in cheap lodgings, always an indication. Wrote a piece for the *Clarion*, got a small sum, thought he could increase it here. I've offered to lend him money, but he won't take it. Stiff-necked, you know."

As he finished speaking, the man in question put his cards down, saying quietly, "I'm done, Gurney."

"Sorry." His opponent pocketed his winnings. He was a tall, red-faced gentleman with a genial expression. "Never thought I could best you in piquet, Herriot, but you had bad cards. However, never despair, up one night down the next. I should know that. So should you."

Mr. Herriot smiled briefly. "I do know, Gurney. I ought to know better, too. Well, I bid you a good evening." From his expression it was impossible to divine whether he had lost or won. He was about to stride from the room when Sir Edwin planted himself before him.

"Did you drop much, Sable?"

He shrugged. "Enough, Edwin."

Sir Edwin frowned. "All?"

Herriot's reply was accompanied by another shrug. "I had bad luck."

"And in consequence you're badly dipped, eh?"

"That should concern none but myself," was the brusque answer.

"I could lend—"

"No. You are uncommon kind, as always, but you know my policy. Never a borrower . . ."

"You have been a lender," Sir Edwin pursued. "It's only right that I—"

"I must go." Mr. Herriot moved around him. "Pray excuse me."

"Wait." Sir Ares stepped forward, flushing as Mr. Herriot eyed him coolly. "I take it, sir, that you are in want of funds?"

"Ares . . ." Sir Edwin muttered warningly.

Mr. Herriot's eyes, a silvery gray, turned frosty. There was a similar chill in his voice as he said softly, "I find that question in damnably poor taste, sir."

Sir Ares's flush deepened but it was not in his nature to abandon the pursuit of anything he desired. "So be it," he continued and then, as if fearing an immediate interruption, began to speak so quickly that the words tumbled from his mouth. "I . . . I have a proposition to offer that I hope you may wish to consider. As you might recall, I spoke to you earlier this evening regarding my journey to Greece. Though my sister and I both speak the language, we need someone who is acquainted with the Turkish tongue and the terrain . . . we have been told that that knowledge is essential. I would pay well for such services."

"Do I understand that you are offering me the position of courier?" Mr. Herriot inquired coldly.

"My dear Ares," Sir Edwin protested. "It is not at all the thing. Sable's not for *hire*."

Unheeding, Sir Ares said doggedly, "We need someone we can trust."

14

"I am sure you do, particularly in that country," Mr. Herriot agreed. "However, it cannot be myself."

He was about to turn away when Sir Ares exclaimed, "Hold! Let me put it another way, then."

"Ares." Sir Edwin's voice held a warning note. "Do you not see that a man of his pride . . ."

As if he had not heard him, Sir Ares continued, "I have done very well at the tables tonight, Mr. Herriot, but—"

"I congratulate you, sir, but I do not quite see . . ." Mr. Herriot interrupted.

Reaching into his pocket, Sir Ares hurriedly extracted his winnings. "I put it to you, Mr. Herriot, I will wager all that I have won on the turn of the cards—two out of three. If you win, you will have something in the nature of two thousand five hundred pounds. If I win, you will come to Greece with us as our companion and our guide. Naturally, you will share our accommodations and you will also be well-recompensed for your services."

Mr. Herriot studied him for a long moment. "Why are you so eager that I accompany you?"

"Because I can think of none better. I do not have the pleasure of your acquaintance but Sir Edwin, whose opinion I respect, speaks of you most highly. You have traveled extensively in the Levant and in Greece. Your books bear testimony to that and to your knowledge of obscure Grecian dialects. Certainly you must know numerous officials, both Turkish and Greek as well as English, is that not true?"

"It is true," Mr. Herriot acknowledged, surveying Sir Ares through narrowed eyes.

"Thus you will be able to pave the way for my sister and myself. I know you do not approve of a female embarking upon such an expedition . . ."

"I do not," Mr. Herriot said firmly.

"No more do I," Sir Ares confessed, "but there is no arguing with her. My parents, who are recently deceased, expressed a wish to have their ashes scattered at the foot of Mount Parnassus. My sister was as devoted to them as I myself, and she is determined to help perform that rite. Come, I pray you will accept the wager. Surely your bad luck cannot last forever."

"That is true enough," Sir Edwin urged. "I believe it a fair proposition and usually you are uncommonly lucky, Sable."

Mr. Herriot favored Sir Ares with another long glance. Then he said lightly, "Since I, too, cannot believe that bad luck can last indefinitely, I shall accept your challenge."

Sir Ares's brown eyes gleamed. "Good," he exclaimed. Moving quickly to a nearby table, he picked up an unopened pack of cards. "Sir Edwin must shuffle." He glanced at Mr. Herriot. "Is that agreeable with you, sir?"

"Quite."

Breaking open the pack, Sir Edwin shuffled and set it down again, inviting first one gentleman and then the other to cut. When that operation had been performed, he said, "Shall we toss a coin to see who has the first turn?"

Sir Ares shook his head. "Mr. Herriot?"

Smiling slightly, Mr. Herriot turned over the card exposing a queen. "Ah," Sir Edwin murmured, "it'll not be easy to better that."

Sir Ares's cut was a ten. "I've not bettered it," he said, a shade of disappointment in his tone.

"Second turn," Sir Edwin announced laconically. Sable?"

Herriot drew a nine and Ares, a knave. On the third turn, Herriot's card was again a queen.

Each of the three men was tense and quiet as Ares slowly drew forth his card. Turning it face up, he displayed a king. Trying in vain to keep an edge of triumph from his tone, he turned to Herriot. "Well, sir . . ."

Herriot's expression was imperturbable as he nodded at Sir Edwin, saying gently, "Well, it seems, my friend, that we were both wrong about luck. Mine holds." His cold glance fell on Sir Ares. "You have won me, sir."

Three days later, Jane Goff, Athena's maid, scurrying down to the servants' hall, met Patrick, Milady Caroline's footman. "Oooh, if there 'asn't been a bit of a dust-up," she confided breathlessly. "H'it do seem h'as h'if we won't be goin' h'after h'all."

"Naow, Patrick said interestedly. "Wot 'appened? Seems to me I 'eard Miss Athena screamin' at 'er brother."

"You did." Jane's smile was ecstatic. "She's 'ad some rare tantrums but this was the worst. It was h'over that Mr. 'Erriot. 'E just left an' she vows she'll not stir a step if e's to come. Now maybe we'll go off to Brighton like sensible folk."

It was a hope that Lady Caroline, sitting on the Egyptian settee in the drawing room, a hand resting on its reptilian coils, fully supported as she watched Athena stride up and down before the fireplace, it having a stretch of space unencumbered by furniture. Mentally, Lady Caroline decried Athena's walk—striding was unladylike—but she forbore to mention it as she watched Sir Ares as he, in turn, studied his sister. Athena had exploded but her

17

brother, on the other hand, was dangerously calm. Either way, it seemed to Lady Caroline as though the projected journey would be summarily canceled.

"I will not travel with that odious man!" Athena flung the words at her brother.

"I suggest that you do not go off into a pet," Sir Ares said icily. "I will not travel without him."

Tempestuous blue eyes met cool brown eyes and locked. Lady Caroline firmed her lips against a small smile. They were trying to outstare each other. She doubted that either would prevail. They were well-matched. Athena had inherited the temperament of her Italian grandmother and Sir Ares, the cold detachment of the man who had married her. Lady Caroline could imagine that their's had been a stormy household. Oddly enough, the brother and sister did not resemble either of their singularly compatible and calm parents. Inadvertently, she glanced apologetically at the twin urns on the mantelshelf, hoping that their spirits were not present and chiding her for the wish that their ashes would eventually find sanctuary in an English cemetery.

"Why do we need him?" Athena demanded. "We both speak the language."

"Neither of us knows Turkish," Sir Ares began and shrugged. "No matter, I have explained why it is very necessary to have a man of his experience with us. It would not be quite so needful if you had not insisted upon coming with me. I imagine that I should fare very well by myself."

"As would I!" his sister retorted. "By myself!"

"You, a female?" he scoffed.

Athena ground her teeth. "I am not helpless, as you well know. Furthermore, even if I was, I should prefer my helplessness to being helped by that . . . that man."

"I admit he is not very conciliating."

"He is rude!"

"Yes. I do not like him, either, but we do not need to like him. Sir Edwin says—"

"Blast Sir Edwin!"

Lady Caroline opened her mouth to chide her niece for such an unladylike expletive and closed it again. Better to let the storm rage to its inevitable conclusion, which could not be in the far distant future.

"Sir Edwin speaks very highly of Mr. Herriot. The man is unquestionably a gentleman. He will not intrude upon us and his services will be invaluable."

"He had the temerity to suggest that I should not come," his sister reminded him. "I presume you heard him."

"He gave his reasons, too. Bandits, bad traveling conditions, uncertain weather, rough terrain—"

"All which I, too, have mentioned, my dear," Lady Caroline interjected.

"None of these was the real reason," Athena snapped. "He did not like me on sight any more than I did him. To be in close quarters with a supercilious creature who looks down his nose at one. . . ."

"You will not be in close quarters with him," Sir Ares interrupted. "I doubt that we shall see much of him on the *Scorpion*. I think, too, that he will keep his distance in Greece. He will be of use in bargaining and—"

"I will not go if he goes," Athena threatened.

Sir Ares smiled. "Excellent. Then I shall—"

"I shall go by myself!" she cried.

"Athena!" Lady Caroline gasped. "Impossible!"

"It is not. I will!"

"You will not," Sir Ares said evenly. "Your guardian will not permit it."

"Guardian?" she echoed. "Who might that be? I do not have a guardian."

"Does she?" Lady Caroline asked hopefully.

"Yes, my dear Aunt, she does." Sir Ares's smile held a quotient of malice. "Papa, knowing your impulsive temperament, my Athena, appointed one."

"I know nothing about that," she cried. "I do not believe you!"

"All the same, until you are twenty-one, you must do his bidding," Sir Ares said.

"Whose bidding? Who is he?" Athena glared at him.

"If you had been biddable, I should not have mentioned it," Sir Ares replied.

"Who is he?"

"Myself," her brother said triumphantly.

"You! You are lying."

"I am not a liar. I have the documents to prove it," he said icily. "Now, my dear sister, I suggest that if you do not want to accompany me to Greece, you and our aunt should go to Brighton or—"

"Bournemouth," Lady Caroline finished, happily. "Yes, that is much the better way."

"You! Athena still looked at Ares doubtfully. "Impossible, you are only two years older than I— how can you be my guardian?"

"Because, my love, I do not go off into tantrums. I am not ridiculously impulsive and I have a modicum of common sense, qualities in which you are sadly lacking as you proved this afternoon."

"That is quite right," Lady Caroline approved, forgetting that she had very deep reservations concerning Ares's character, too. "Your Papa made a wise decision."

"Actually," Sir Ares confided, "I should have preferred not to have the charge. I told him as much when he proposed it."

"When did he propose it? He could not have known he was about to die?" Athena cried.

"As to that—" Sir Ares's gaze darkened— "it was shortly before he took that fence on the field."

"He had a premonition!" Lady Caroline exclaimed. "I have heard of such things."

"Yes . . . a premonition," her nephew said stiffly.

"Oh!" Athena's eyes filled with tears and she sank down in a chair, hiding her face in her hands. Suddenly, it was all back with her, their father's death on the hunting field just three months after their mother had succumbed to pneumonia.

Sir Ares knelt quickly by her side, putting his arms around her, holding her tightly against him. "I did not mean that you should know it, dear," he said regretfully.

"How he must have loved her," Athena whispered.

"Yes," he stroked her hair. "Yet, I wish I'd not told you."

"You should have told me. You should not have shouldered the burden alone." She looked into his troubled face. "Nor shall you go alone to Greece. I will come with you." With a slight grimace she added, "I expect I can avoid that man, if I put my mind to it."

"I am sure you can, my dearest. I know that I shall make the effort, too," he said, giving her an affectionate hug. "If we did not need him, I should not have insisted. And I am glad that you are coming."

That Sir Ares's sentiment was not echoed by the object of his argument with his sister would not have surprised him, though possibly, he might have been taken aback had he known the extent of the aversion in which Mr. Herriot held the young woman in question. Indeed, much as Athena had stridden up and down her aunt's drawing room, Mr. Herriot, in describing the recent interview with his new employers to Sir Edwin Calthrope, paced the considerable length of the latter's elegant library.

"Spoiled and sulky," he rasped. "A great gawk of a female. I shouldn't be surprised if she weighed in at eleven stone . . . with huge glaring eyes, a Roman countenance and a determination like unto Cornelia, the mother of the Gracchi, I have no doubt. She was all defiance when I told her Greece was hardly the place for a young lady unacquainted with the hardships of travel in that part of the world. You tell me that Eames cried off—I thought it a dastardly action until I met her. Now I cannot wonder at it! The marvel to me is that he had the courage to propose in the first place. I should as soon wed a Barbary ape."

"Money," Sir Edwin said succinctly. "He was much in need of it until his uncle had the grace to die."

"Had she three times the fortune she possesses, I should not want her."

"Come," Sir Edwin soothed. "She is not quite that dreadful. To any eye but yours, she appears quite lovely. Furthermore, I have had conversation with her and I believe her to be shy and ill-at-ease in society which might account for her . . . slightly forbidding manner. Too, I have the impression that she is extremely intelligent."

"Preserve me from 'extremely intelligent' women! They are bound to be officious. She and her brother are two of a kind—impetuous and immature. I do not look forward to being thrust into their company for months on end. I vow I do not know how I shall be able to stomach it."

"No doubt, you would prefer debtors' prison?"

"No doubt but that I should," Mr. Herriot glared at his friend. "Lord, Lord, why did I let you persuade me to gamble with that young whelp the other night? My luck was out, I should have known from past experience that it would not improve!"

"On the contrary, I am of the opinion that your luck has much improved. In spite of your avowed preference for the felicities of the Fleet, I cannot think that a man of your touch, loving freedom as you do, could bear the confinement of that musty prison. You do not need to be always in that girl's society or in her brother's, either. You can discharge your duties and remain by yourself." Sir Edwin smiled slightly. "However, who knows, you might even come to like her."

"As I like my stepmother!" Mr. Herriot shot him an angry glance, the while his hands clenched and twisted in a strangling motion.

Sir Edwin's own glance was sympathetic. It was on the tip of his tongue to proffer some advice, but a look into Mr. Herriot's brooding eyes quelled that particular wish. Instead, he patted him on the shoulder saying cordially, "Come, it's time and past time that we supped. I should like your opinion on the wine I've lately imported from Dijon."

Two

Athena opened her eyes cautiously. Then, almost without volition, they widened. Rather than the pitching and the tossing she had endured nearly every day since she had left England, there was just the hint of movement in the small cabin, a sort of gentle rocking. She should have known that, she reasoned, because the horrid feeling inside her had vanished. Though she was still conscious of weakness, fatigue and the memory of something very unpleasant that had taken place during the previous evening, but which she could not quite recall for the moment, there was no longer any of the dreadful nausea which had claimed her for most of the voyage. She frowned. She was extremely annoyed with her rebellious constitution that, independent of her strong will, had reacted very badly to the ship's motion. She exhaled a short angry breath. Several times in the past weeks, Mr. Le Strange, the ship's doctor, a man with a very positive way of speaking, had assured her that once she had acquired her "sea legs" she would no longer suffer from *mal de mer*. Several times he had been wrong. A large wave, and there had been many of these, had only to set the vessel to heaving and she would be prostrated again. Her frown deepened. She, who had always imagined that she would be an excellent sailor, able to remain on deck in all weathers, had experienced her first queasy feeling at the very commencement of the voyage; she had gone on experiencing this sickness all the way to Gibraltar, their first stop, and during most of the way to Palermo, their second. She had been far too unwell to go exploring in either port and she had feared that she would be similarly incapacitated in Malta, where, she guessed, they must have dropped anchor now. She shuddered slightly. They were due to change ships at Malta and sail on to Zante, which was one of the Ionian Islands and, after that, they would arrive in Patras on the Greek mainland. It had been an itinerary worked out by Mr. Herriot. On paper it had appeared extremely exciting. In addition to inheriting her parents' fascination with and reverence for Greece, she had always longed to visit strange ports. Now, due to her continuing indisposition, she could only contemplate the next two weeks with a shuddering memory of those that had gone before.

She moved restlessly in her bed. If only someone else had displayed similar symptoms, she would not have been so disturbed. However, neither Ares nor Jane nor Mr. Herriot had been afflicted. It was not that she wished any one of them to suffer—but the fact that Mr. Herriot must be thinking that her condition bore out his opinion that she should have remained behind in some discreet watering place on England's shores galled her. Of course, it little mattered what a courier thought, and bet or no bet, that was what he was doing and being paid for it, too! Still, throughout the voyage, she had been wishing that she had adhered to her original contention that, if Ares chose to avail himself of Mr. Herriot's services, she, Athena, would travel to Greece by herself. It would have been easy enough. Once her brother had gone ahead with Mr. Herriot, he could hardly remain behind to forbid her leaving, too. She ground her teeth. It would be lovely to be free of the hateful Mr. Herriot. As she had told Ares, she had disliked him on sight, but that she had blamed partially on her newly formed distrust of all men. However, the feelings she now entertained for Mr. Herriot were far more specific. She did not merely dislike him, she loathed him. This in spite of the fact that she had seen very little of him in the last weeks. Yet, when she had seen him . . .

Unwillingly she cast her mind back to her first moments aboard the brig o'war so aptly named *H.M.S. Scorpion.* It had been her greatest wish at that time to prove Mr. Herriot wrong. Waiting on the quay, she had imagined letting him see her standing fearlessly in the bow of the vessel, her black locks caught by the wild-wet winds—it was an image she had culled from a novel entitled *Hermione or: Buffeted by Fate,* which she had bought at the Minerva Press. Hermione had been wonderfully at home on shipboard and one of her favorite spots was the bow. Accordingly, Athena had assumed the stance immediately she had come on board only to collapse and lose all of a large midday meal over the side, only moments after they had caught the sea winds that had borne them forth from the harbor.

Wincing, Athena closed her eyes, but there was no shutting out the image that remained—of herself sobbing, hiccoughing and being ignominiously deposited in her cabin by a pair of sailors, who were trying, unsuccessfully, to hide their grins. They had been overseen by Mr. Herriot, who had not been grinning, of course, but there had been no mistaking the chill hauteur stamped on his features. Obviously, he had held her in as much contempt as she him and certainly no one could have been more indifferent to her miserable plight. Worse yet, his low opinion of her had rubbed off on her brother—as witness his attitude when he had come to see her last night.

"I understand you're more the thing, my dear," he had said.

"I am certainly not myself," she had muttered resentfully. "Furthermore, I am not looking forward to tomorrow, when we must change to that pol ... pola ..."

"Polacca," Ares had clarified. "Quite a nice little vessel, Mr. Herriot assures me. He has sailed on her before."

"Little vessel," Athena had groaned. "On these terrible seas, we shall be tossed about like a piece of driftwood. Why does that creature insist that we change ships?"

"But you know we must change," Ares had raised his eyebrows. "The Scorpion sails no further than Malta. Come, my dear, we've only two more ports to touch. In another three weeks, given favorable winds, we should be at our destination."

Rather than being conciliating, he had been extremely annoyed when Athena had rolled about in bed, wailing, "Three weeks ... three more weeks at sea. I shall *dieeee*."

"You shan't die," he had replied in a cold tone. "My. Herriot says that with a little effort, you could be on your feet now. All you need do is eat."

"Eat?" she had shrieked. "Eat ... when the very smell of food is enough to ... He is completely heartless and so are you! Have you no consideration for my feelings at all?"

Ares's eyebrows had shot up and come down in a frown. "I have tried to be considerate," he had told her in cold accents that could easily rival those of Mr. Herriot, "but I find a month of catering to the whims of an imaginary invalid damned boring, as does everyone else who is forced to minister to you." Much to her indignation, he had stalked out, closing the door sharply behind him.

It had not helped matters at all when, before Athena had calmed down, Jane entered bearing a tray on which was a repast of tea and toast, recommended, she had informed her mistress, by Sir Ares.

Of course, she had angrily refused it, launching into a denunciation of her brother and the man who now appeared to be his mentor. However, it had seemed to her that while Jane had listened dutifully to her plaints, there had been an abstraction in her attitude that suggested a total lack of interest in her mistress's suffering. Athena's face burned. Here was the unpleasantness which had passed from her mind. It was back and she would as lief it had remained buried. It revealed a side of her nature she had not known she possessed.

Glaring at Jane, she had accused, "You do not care. No one cares how miserable I feel. You are totally indifferent."

Jane's answer had been extremely unfortunate. Placing the tray on the table beside Athena's bed, she had said, "Yes, Miss."

"Yes!" Athena had cried. "You've not been listening to me! You've not heard one word I've uttered. Or, if you have, then you are impertinent, and I tell you I shall not tolerate such behavior in a servant. You are forthwith dismissed." She had punctuated her words by hurling the tray on the floor at Jane's feet.

Of course, she had meant neither the words nor the action. Jane was a sweet girl, who had been with her for three years—she was an excellent maid with a remarkable talent for dressing Athena's long and almost unmanageable hair. Numerous friends had told her she was lucky to have Jane. They had also offered Jane higher wages in an effort to coax the girl from her side. Jane had always loyally refused. It had not been Jane, however, who had precipitated the incident, it had been Mr. Herriot's unfeeling attitude as conveyed by Ares; but whatever the cause, the effect had been the same. Jane had given her one horrified glance and dashed from the cabin. She had not come back. No one had come and, as a reminder of her tantrum, Athena, peeping at the floor, perceived scattered pieces of toast and a plate. The teapot and mug, she guessed, were probably beneath the bed.

From force of habit, she reached for the bell-pull beside her, only to remember that there was none and that, for the duration of her illness, Jane had been in the habit of coming to see her of an early morning—so soon upon her awakening as to make her believe the girl had a sixth sense. Jane had always asked what she wanted and, without being requested had tenderly smoothed Athena's hair and bathed a brow which, though not actually fevered, had always felt the better for that kind attention. Athena swallowed a large lump in her throat. Jane had been more than patient and she had been horrid and ungrateful. Last night, she had been more than horrid, she had been cruelly unjust. Tears pricked her eyes—eyes which blinked against the brightness of the porthole. With a little shock, she realized that it was no longer early morning—the sun must have risen several hours ago. Obviously Jane was still sulking and it behooved her to apologize. She wanted to apologize. She would give her maid something —a jewel or the lavender gown she had admired so extravagantly while it was being fitted. She had not been covetous. Jane was never covetous like some ladies' maids who purposely spilled things on garments and represented them to their mistresses as being hopelessly spoiled, only to appear in them on their walking-out days. Jane was a paragon.

Athena, thinking over Ares's comments of the previous evening, had an uncomfortable suspicion that he was right. She *had* given in to herself too much. In fact, her retreat to her cabin and even her prolonged illness might have been a way of making matters difficult for him because of his insistence upon the unwanted presence of Mr. Herriot. She wished that that particular explanation had not occurred to her. She did not want it to be accurate. It presented a most unflattering image. Reluctantly, she recalled something else, her parents, laughing over the machinations of one Dimity Sorrel, a neighbor. Mrs. Sorrel, a fragile, pink-and-white blonde, with a lisping baby voice—a type Athena particularly detested—was given to fainting away every time her long-suffering spouse gainsaid one of her wishes. She had been, her mother had not hesitated to say, "a domestic tyrant" of the very worst sort. A sixteen-year-old Athena had agreed, pronouncing the said Mrs. Sorrel a "weak-kneed, poor-spirited female." Now she was faced with the uncomfortable suspicion that, unconsciously, she had aped Mrs. Sorrel.

"I'm not a poor-spirited female," she whispered.

"It's just that..." She cringed away from yet another unwelcome memory, the dark, shamed countenance of Eames as he had jerkily told her that he was withdrawing his offer. Then, coming so close upon that telling blow, to encounter another man, who also held her in such poor regard... Yet to have vented all that upon poor Jane was inexcusable. Her mother, who had always treated her domestic staff with the greatest kindness and consideration, would have been horrified. She, Athena, was also horrified.

Impulsively, she slipped out of bed only to have the room circle around her in a most unsettling manner. She staggered back, falling on her bed and clutching one of its iron posts, steadying herself until her head stopped behaving in that untoward way. Still she was not entirely displeased. Her dizziness suggested that she was not really very well. Consequently, she did have an excuse for remaining in bed and also for her untoward behavior! Yet, no sooner did this comforting reassurance arise in her mind than she caught sight of a piece of toast on the floor. Involuntarily, she seized it and bit into it. It was very dry; but it tasted like ambrosia! Falling to her knees, Athena retrieved the rest of the toast, devouring it ravenously. Much to her amazement, it did make her feel better, but she wanted something more than toast; she was extremely hungry. She had not had much in the way of solid food these last weeks. Her cheeks burned. It was no good being dishonest with herself. Her present weakness was not the result of her illness. Her brother had been quite right and Mr. Herriot, too, blast him! She had only needed to eat!

There was a tap on the door. No doubt it was

poor Jane and she should have the lavender dress and a cashmere shawl as well! In a small, shamed voice, Athena called, "Come in, Jane, dear."

The door was opened but it was not Jane, who stood on the threshold, it was Ares, regarding her with a mixture of anger and contempt. "Jane is not coming. I am sure I need not explain why."

"Oh, dear . . . I expect she is very angry with me. I did not mean . . ."

"On the contrary." Ares shut the door and came to stand at Athena's bed. "Jane is not angry with you. In fact, she is delighted. You see, she had not quite known how to tell you what she had in mind. Indeed, because of your illness, I doubt that she would have told you at all; but fortunately you made it extremely easy for her."

"Easy?" Athena repeated with a strange throb in the region of her throat. Suddenly she was fearful though she could not have explained why. Her brother obviously could. "What are you saying?" she demanded nervously.

"Jane is leaving—or rather, has left—your service."

A hand to her pulsing throat, Athena cried, "B-But she cannot . . . I did not mean it . . . Surely she knows . . ."

"I think," Ares interrupted, "that under ordinary circumstances, she might have overlooked your most reprehensible behavior, but William Hooks would not allow it."

"William Hooks? Who is William Hooks?"

"Able Seaman Hooks has fallen head over heels in love with the fair Jane and she with him. It was into his comforting arms that she fled last night—he being directly outside the door. He carried your tray

33

up from the galley. She'll be marrying him directly upon returning to England. She's going back with him on *The Scorpion.*"

"B-But she cannot leave me!" Athena wailed. "What shall I ever do without her . . . and if she is going to wait to marry him . . . why?"

"You know why, Athena. Jane is a girl with pride, not a slave. She's cared for you very faithfully these last weeks. She did not deserve such treatment. I wonder what Mama—"

"Oh, do stop!" Athena slipped from the bed and came to him. "Mama would have been very angry with me and well I know it! I have been angry with myself. You cannot think I meant to turn on Jane. It was just that . . ." She paused. She had been about to mention Mr. Herriot, but his name stuck in her throat and besides, Ares was in no mood to heed such confidences. They would only anger him. She said, "It was my temper. I was not myself last night. You know I am not usually so difficult. It is that I am not used to being ill."

Ares's gaze softened. He could well believe that she was speaking the truth. Nearly three weeks of abstinence had told on her, too. From being slightly plump, she was now far too thin, almost haggard-looking. He had a feeling that Mr. Herriot who, with Hooks, had united in soothing weeping Jane, might not agree with him; but he was positive Athena had not meant it. Doubtless, Jane knew it, too, being accustomed to Athena's vagaries, these three years past. His sister did have a tempestuous nature but her outbursts of temper were over very quickly and he had a suspicion that Jane had never been the loser by them. In fact, he would not be surprised if the bride-clothes she would bring to Mr. Hooks

34

were greatly augmented by reason of Athena's numerous conciliatory gifts. He patted her shoulder, "I am afraid there's no help for it, my girl. However, perhaps we can find you another servant in Malta."

"I do not want another! I love Jane. Can I say nothing ... ?"

Ares regarded her doubtfully. "You can try. I will send her to you."

"She's always been sensible before ..." Athena murmured.

"Before William Hooks."

"But she cannot throw herself away on a sailor!" Athena cried. "They have dreadful reputations. Has no one warned her?"

"You were ill." Ares winked.

"You may make light of it, but sailors . . ."

"I am aware of their reputations." He added meaningfully, "But not all sailors nor all men are the same, Athena. You must learn to make distinctions. And, if I were you, I should not be so quick to proffer advice, not in this instance."

"I have her best interests at heart," Athena said.

"Have you?"

Meeting his quizzical gaze, she said earnestly, "I do. Honestly, I do."

She had spoken the truth. She said as much to Jane, to no appreciable effect. Though her ex-servant forgave her readily, as she always had before, nothing could make her change her plans. "I 'ave given my word, Miss Athena," she repeated stubbornly to each argument Athena had advanced. In the end, a saddened Athena gave her the lavender dress and the cashmere shawl as a wedding present.

Some two hours later, Athena had an opportunity to see the engaged pair. Jane looked very fetching in the lavender dress. The young man with her, a sturdy, stocky youth with sun-bleached yellow hair and a sea-reddened complexion lit by very blue eyes, gazed at her with a proud smile. Mr. Herriot was also smiling, though, Athena noted, his gray eyes remained sober. He was walking near the couple while she, leaning on Ares's arm, strolled slowly behind them up the main street of Valetta, the capital of Malta. Though she had had a substantial noonday meal, she was still a little weak, and her mirror had told her she looked her very worst. In addition to the fact that her favorite blue lutestring gown hung on her wasted frame, her skin was a pale yellow and there were dark circles under her eyes.

Notwithstanding the fact that a mollified Jane had worked hard on her hair, it, too, was lank and lusterless. She had caught Mr. Herriot staring at her and had guessed that her changed appearance must have startled him. Yet it had not moved him to any expressions of sympathy. Indeed, he had regarded her with an icy contempt that showed her that he had been informed about the incident that had robbed her of her servant. She was also certain that he believed it to be one in a long line of tantrums rather than an isolated episode. Quite possibly he believed that she had beat Jane regularly. She longed to tell him that, though she had lost her temper with the girl on other occasions, never until the previous evening had she actually thrown anything at her. Yet, what would be the use of that and why did it matter to her? If he chose to think of her as a violent-tempered and cruel female, let him! His opinion did not matter, not in the least!

"Not in the *least* least," she muttered through clenched teeth.

"I beg your pardon, my dear?" Ares murmured.

"Nothing," she answered self-consciously.

" 'Tis known that the French yet covet this island and Napoleon is eager to reconquer it." Mr. Herriot had been speaking to Mr. Hooks but, evidently mindful of his duties as a guide, he had made his way back to a point between the two couples. "It is a highly strategic spot. Look." He came to a stop, pointing to a statue of St. Michael subduing Satan; the sculpture was on a pedestal at a cross street. The four of them obediently paused to stare at it.

"Oooh, it's ever so nice," Jane commented. "It must be very old."

"Very," Mr. Herriot corroborated. "Easily three hundred years. And the Knights of Malta . . ."

"Oh, look, Athena!" Ares spoke over Mr. Herriot's words. "Mama mentioned that statue." He laughed. "She said it had a silly look on its face. And it does."

Catching Mr. Herriot's cold glance, Athena guessed that he had not been pleased at the interruption. She made a point of saying, "Indeed it does. Also the Devil looks mighty uncomfortable; imagine having a foot on your back for three hundred years!"

Mr. Herriot turned to Jane. "There's a tradition that St. Paul visited this shore."

"St. Paul?" Jane breathed. "Did 'e?"

"Yes, it's thought he landed on the other side of the island. He was being borne a prisoner to Rome and the ship was wrecked. 'And when they were escaped, they knew the island was Melita,' " he quoted.

"Melita?" Sir Ares asked.

"The Biblical name of Malta." Mr. Herriot explained.

"'E killed a snake didn't 'e?" Mr. Hooks remarked. "H'I seem to remember Parson sayin' as much."

Mr. Herriot nodded. "It was a miracle. 'And when Paul had gathered a bundle of sticks, and laid them on the fire, there came a viper out of the heat, and fastened on his hand.

"'And when the barbarians saw the venomous beast hang on his hand, they said among themselves, "No doubt this man is a murderer, whom though he hath escaped the sea, yet vengeance suffereth not to live."

"'And he shook off the beast into the fire, and felt no harm.

"'Howbeit they looked when he should have swollen, or fallen down dead suddenly; but after they had looked a great while, they changed their minds, and said that he was a god.'"

"Fancy you rememberin' all that scripture," Jane marveled.

Mr. Herriot's smile was slightly twisted. "I had a pious Scotswoman for a nurse."

"And the devil can quote scripture..." The thought floated through Athena's mind. She leaned against the base of the statue. Unlike the others, she had not been impressed by Mr. Herriot's Biblical knowledge, but rather by the chill tone of voice in which he had delivered the verses. Everything about him was so cold—from his frosty voice to his features, which, though handsome enough, had an almost sculptured look. He might have been a statue himself. His eyes were cold, too. That had been her first impression of him. Confined to her cabin for the

38

last weeks, she had forgotten that initial impact; now it returned in full force. It was amazing how much she disliked him! The idea of spending more time in his company was as appalling as it was unavoidable. Her lip curled as she remembered her brother's elation over the securing of Mr. Herriot's services: "A lucky turn of the cards."

"*Lucky*," she whispered bitterly. All her pleasure in the journey was spoiled. In fact, it seemed to her that with the advent of Mr. Herriot, she and Ares had come under a dark star. There had been that stormy crossing, her illness, the loss of Jane and . . . there would be more. She shivered. She was suddenly sure of that, so sure of it that she wanted to warn her brother, now, this very instant before it was too late! Impulsively, she turned in his direction —then gazed blankly ahead. He was not there and nor were Jane, Mr. Hooks or Mr. Herriot. While she had been lost in thought, they had gone on without her. Hurriedly she started to follow them—but *was* she following them? They had been at a cross street and she had no idea in which direction they had gone. And she had not realized that there were so many people on the street. Now, as she tried to see if she might catch a glimpse of them—her height would stand her in good stead there since the Maltese, in common with the Italians, all seemed of less than average height—she found herself in a dense crowd. Nuns, priests, soldiers and civilians were milling around her. The air was filled with the cries of beggars and hawkers and with the incomprehensible language of the people. It was also very hot. Odd, how all of this had escaped her before, when Ares had been at her side. Someone brushed against her: she had to move ahead; she could not stand still in the midst of this great crowd.

As she started to walk, the weakness of which she had been conscious before seemed to grow worse and the sun was really dreadfully hot. Her sunshade, a flimsy, ruffled trifle, offered very little protection, and her bonnet of light woven straw sufficed beneath an English sky; but here in Malta ... Really, she was feeling most unwell! She frowned. She was not going to give into the demands of her debilitated body. Mr. Herriot would despise her the more, and truthfully she despised herself, deploring her lack of strength.

Setting her jaw and clenching her teeth she strode on ahead. Her aunt did not approve of her taking such long steps, she recalled that, but ... if only it were not so hot! She had a feeling that the sun was devouring all the air—sucking it out of the atmosphere so that there was little left and that little must be shared by the great masses of people around her and there was not enough, not nearly enough! Her foot caught in a depression on the street and she fell heavily. Gravel bit into her palms. People crowded around her and the air was going. Everyone was talking at once and she could not understand anything. Then two arms encircled her. A stranger had seized her—a tall man, who towered over her. Whimpering with fright, she struggled against the strong grip.

"Miss Penrose, let me help you up, please."

She tensed. The words were courteous enough but the tone in which they were uttered was fraught with annoyance. "Mr. Herriot!" She twisted about to see his dark-browed countenance only inches away from hers, his gray eyes, no longer cool, but alight with anger.

"Oh," she murmured, clutching his arm and, as

he pulled her to her feet, she added reluctantly, "Thank you. I fell."

"Yes." He nodded, saying curtly, "Did you hurt yourself?"

She was aware of assorted bruises and smarts as well as an ever increasing weakness, but she had no intention of telling him that. "Not in the least," she said valiantly. "I was only clumsy."

"I am glad you were not hurt," he commented in a tone so indifferent as to belie his statement. "Miss Penrose," he continued, "I must ask you please not to wander off in these places. You were fortunate that I was able to find you. You might not always be so fortunate."

"I . . . you . . ." It was on the tip of her tongue to explain that it was they who left her behind, but on looking into his face, she was silenced by the expression in his eyes. With a shock, she realized that however much she resented and disliked him, the feeling he entertained for her was one of sheer hatred. Her sense of animosity suddenly changed to one of fear. He looked, she thought, almost murderous!

"A man of honor." The phrase was large in Mr. Herriot's mind as he assisted Miss Penrose up the street to where her brother was anxiously waiting. If it were not for his vaunted honor, he would have returned to England with *The Scorpion*, too. All that he had anticipated upon meeting Miss Penrose had come to pass—though rather than being headstrong and determined, she was obviously going to be a dead weight. He had not suspected her of the weakness she had demonstrated during the last three weeks. However, it was all of a piece with her ill-temper. A vivid impression of her poor little maid

41

dashing out of the cabin, her gown splashed with the hot tea that had been hurled at her, came to his mind.

If she had been his sister, he would have put her over his knee—but her brother was obviously used to indulging her follies. He, Sable Herriot, was not and the pair of them would learn that rather quickly—that is, if they intended to continue availing themselves of his services, which, judging from Miss Penrose's dark looks, they might not. He was quite aware that her dislike of him had increased; but that, he reasoned, was all to the good. There had been a time when he had guided a husband and wife through the Levant, only to have the lady act in a manner that had proved singularly embarrassing. He . . . There was a small groan in his ear. He turned quickly just in time to catch Miss Penrose as she toppled forward in a faint.

The sound that escaped Mr. Herriot as he lifted her in his arms might have been an exclamation of concern—but to a Maltese citizen who passed him at that moment, it had sounded far more like a snarl.

Three

Athena, clad in a white cotton gown cut in the still fashionable Grecian mold, stood in the stern of the ship, watching the receding port of Zante or Zakynthos as Mr. Herriot insisted on terming it—that being the island's Greek name. If her dark hair were not being whipped back by the winds in true *Hermione* style, some of it had escaped its confining ribbons and swirled about her face, causing her no end of annoyance. What had stirred her imagination on the printed page was not nearly so effective in actuality. Her locks kept flying into her mouth or plastering themselves against her eyes. Still, feeling the sting of the spray on her face and breathing in the salt air, she did feel exhilarated. She might have been completely happy if Mr. Herriot were not somewhere aboard the *Apollo*, which was the name of the small, Greek-manned polacca they had taken from Malta to Zante and on which they were presently bound for Patras.

"Greece!" she whispered.

In the last week and a half, it had become a magical word again and the sense of pending danger she had experienced on Malta was quite gone. That, she was sure, was due to her physical condition. Since that disastrous moment when she had fainted on the street in Malta, her health had improved amazingly. Though she had not regained the weight she had lost, she was eating three meals a day—on shipboard! Despite the discrepancy in size between the *Apollo* and *The Scorpion*, she had not been ill, not once. Though Ares attributed her recovery to the fact that having finally acquired her sea legs, she could not lose them, she had a private conviction that it was due mainly to her absolutely iron determination to prove to Mr. Herriot that she was no longer the vaporish female, who had fallen into his unwilling arms her first morning ashore. She drew and expelled a long hissing breath and knew her cheeks were flushed. Each time she thought of that episode she had these reactions. The idea of being at such a disadvantage before a man who hated her was particularly appalling. Though it was impossible to discern from his attitude whether she had succeeded in softening the bad impression she had made, at least there had been no repetition of that action.

She had done a great deal of walking in the beautiful port of Zante, making sure, however that she stayed in the vicinity of Ares or Mr. Herriot. Unlike her brother, she had listened carefully to Mr. Herriot's discourses on the history of the island. Ares had confided that he found them too detailed for his liking, reminding him strongly of the droners at Cambridge. It was an attitude based, she was sure, on his resentment of Mr. Herriot's efforts to keep him from committing such indiscretions as flirting with the veiled women who padded after their Turkish husbands in the port or venturing into small, noisome cafés where he might easily have been robbed and murdered. He had been furious when his courier had told him coldly, "An English-man is not God in Islam, Sir Ares." Much as she disliked Mr. Herriot, she could agree that Ares was making an error in not following his advice. Reminded that he had brought the man with him to provide that very advice, he had told her sharply, "I did not engage him as my bear-leader or my commanding officer. He oversteps his authority; he forgets that he has no authority save what I choose to allow him."

She had found that reply both inconsistent and overbearing. "You speak as if he's your servant. That is wrong."

"I shouldn't defend him, if I were you. He has scant respect for you."

"Nor I for him, but what is right is right. He is not a servant and he does know more about this part of the world than either of us. You should heed him."

He did know a great deal about it, for, as became a man who had written books on his travels, he was very well-informed. It occurred to her that if he were not so unpleasant, she could have admired his intelligence. As it was, she still yearned for the time when they might part company forever!

"Ah, Mademoiselle, you are the very picture of a young Amazon—Hippolyta herself," someone breathed into her ear.

Athena looked down to meet the entranced gaze of Mahmood Enver, a high-ranking Turkish official, who had embarked at Zante and like themselves was bound for Patras, where he had one of several homes. Since Ares had chartered the vessel, he had not been obliged to allow him passage, but Mr. Herriot having explained that it was well to keep on the good side of the Turks, Ares had agreed. Enver was a short, dark, plump man, dressed in flowing robes and wearing a tassled fez. Hardly prepossessing as to features, he had a pompous self-satisfied air about him. Watching him come on board with a retinue of servants and slaves, Athena had noted with considerable distaste that, rather than walking, he had strutted. He was even less appealing at close quarters, being heavily doused with a cloying Oriental scent. His eyes, she saw with aversion, were roaming rapidly up and down her body, making her uncomfortably aware that her damp gown revealed more of her shape than was seemly.

Giving him a cold and quelling stare, she was about to turn away, when he said quickly, "But perhaps I am being unmannerly in addressing you. I do not mean to be so; it is only that I have a question to ask you." Before she could respond, he continued, "It is that I wonder, shall you be joining those who take from the ground and from the monuments artifacts to send back to your great country?"

"No." Athena frowned. In common with many of London's citizens, she had gone to view the collection that Lord Elgin had sent back from Greece some two and a half years earlier. She had marveled over figures from the Parthenon pediments and parts of friezes from that same temple as well as lovely caryatid columns, numerous beautiful Greek heads and other sculpture, acquisitions of which the British Museum was naturally very proud. Until she had overheard Mr. Herriot discussing what he contemptuously called "Elgin's rape," she had not known that the Scottish earl had overseen the removal of more than a hundred of those same marbles, pieces that belonged by rights to the people whose ancestors had carved and erected them. It was, she recalled, another of the times when she had discovered herself to be in complete agreement with the courier. The recollection prompted her to add sharply, "I should not wish to have anything to do with that."

"Ah." The little Turk rolled his small brown eyes. "That is an intelligent response. No doubt you have heard that we Turks are, officially, much against such ... removals." He lowered his voice. "Yet were I to learn of such an expedition and subsequent discovery, I should be extremely grateful for that information. The sales, as you no doubt are aware, are often held in Zante. I, myself, attended one, a week since—but unfortunately, I arrived too late to make a purchase. Not all the sculptures that are found are of the same high quality. Mr. Herriot could tell you that."

"Mr. Herriot?" she questioned.

"Mr. Sable Herriot is very well-informed as to the value of certain sculptures." Mahmood Enver smiled. His dark glance, encountering Athena's puzzled stare, turned knowing. "You must sometime ask him about his . . . many *rewarding* transactions."

"I am not in the least interested in Mr. Herriot's transactions!" Athena replied coldly. "Now, if you will excuse me, I must return to my cabin."

She was trembling with rage when she gained her bed. Sitting down, she glared at the chair beside it, seeing in her mind's eye Mr. Herriot seated in a similar chair, coldly castigating the self-proclaimed archaeologists who were pillaging Greece of her antiquities. He had had another name for them—he had called them thieves. She was not surprised at his duplicity, she told herself, only to decide a moment later that, on the contrary, she was surprised. Unpleasant though he was, she had believed him honest; but to deliberately engage in the practice of selling artifacts while loudly inveighing against it suggested a depth of hypocrisy that she hated to find in a fellow countryman. To say that she was disappointed in him would not be true. It was not disappointment that she was feeling, it was disgust and, worse than that, distrust!

She remembered her brother's gleeful account of how he had won Mr. Herriot's services. Now she wondered if that dreadful man had not deliberately cheated when he had based so much on the turn of a card. It was quite possible that he had played *his* cards very well, gaining a free passage back to Greece so that he could pursue his nefarious trade. Athena ground her teeth. She longed to call him to account but that presented difficulties since she seldom saw him. He did not even take his meals with them, preferring the society of Aristides Pappamichaels, the captain of the *Apollo*, and his officers. Since he had sailed on her before, he was very friendly with the master. It occurred to her that he had gone to quite a bit of trouble to locate and charter the vessel. He had told Ares that there was no other ship as seaworthy and no other crew as dependable. Dependable in what way? Was it possible that Pappamichaels and his men were in the habit of helping Mr. Herriot transport his "discoveries" and purchase? Another even more disturbing thought slipped into her mind; it was also possible that she and Ares were his dupes—used as masks for his *sub rosa* activities. That supposition was enough to bring her forth from her cabin in search of her brother. He must, she reasoned angrily, know the character of the man upon whom he was depending to bring them safely through Greece!

Never had Ares resembled his paternal grandfather Sir William Penrose so much as when he rounded on his sister, who at that moment was the very picture of Bianca Coronaro, her paternal grandmother, as with heaving bosom and defiant eyes, she glared at him while he said icily, "You took the word on all this from that slimy little Turk?"

"It sounds logical enough to me!" Athena fumed.

"No, there's nothing logical about your thinking when it comes to Mr. Herriot. It is pure feminine unreason."

"You do not like him, either!"

"True, but I cannot believe he cheated his way on board. I know nothing about him—but I do know Sir Edwin and he did the shuffling and cutting of the cards."

She was not to be downed by this piece of logic. "I tell you, I know that person is going to lead us into trouble."

"How do you know? Have you, in common with Apollo's Pythonesses, been gifted with divine revelation? You are being ridiculous and what's more, unpatriotic."

"Unpatriotic!?"

"Taking the word of that fat and greasy Levantine over that of a true-born Englishman—merely because you have a prejudice against him."

Her bosom heaved. "I am not so small-minded!"

"You are in this regard and it will not do! We need him to take us to Delphi—so both of us will just have to bear with him."

"How do you know that either of us will ever reach Delphi?" she demanded darkly.

Ares laughed. "You read too many novels, my dear."

"Oh!" Athena had a great deal more to say, but she could see that her brother was not in the mood to listen. Giving him a quelling glance, she hurried out of the cabin. In her headlong rush, however, she stumbled and was righted by someone who caught her quickly, just as she seemed in danger of falling full-length on the slippery, sea-washed deck. Raising her eyes to thank the seaman who had rescued her, she encountered Mr. Herriot's chill and, it seemed to her, sneering countenance. However, as he had saved her from a possibly painful tumble, she said, though most ungraciously, "Thank you."

He muttered something in reply, but she did not hear him, being in the companionway by then. On reaching her cabin again, she was trembling once more with frustration. If only, she thought crossly, she could have given him a cold stare, one that would have revealed the utter contempt in which she held him! Unfortunately, the circumstances attendant upon that particular meeting precluded such an action. Furthermore, she was not at all sure that such a look would have had the desired effect, since utter contempt was her habitual expression whenever they were faced with each other.

"The sea upon which Ulysses sailed ... the lands he touched," Ares said, standing beside his sister at the railing of the *Apollo*, as they gazed excitedly upon the approaching mainland.

She laughed. "Zante was part of Ulysses's kingdom but you did not wax near so poetical over that," she said teasingly.

"But this is Greece proper." Ares's dark eyes were gleaming. "Given the favor of Aeolus and his winds, we should be in Patras by late this afternoon. We might be on our way to Delphi in another day."

"Another day . . . fancy!" Athena smiled at him. Ares was looking particularly handsome that afternoon. With his waving wheat-gold hair and his regular features, he looked not unlike the Greeks of old. Though she would never have admitted it, she was disappointed in what she had seen of the present Greeks. Not one of them resembled those noble heads that Lord Elgin had despatched to London, nor did they possess the proud carriage and beautiful bodies; being, on the whole, short and swart, not unlike the larger part of the conquering Turks. Certainly, her brother with his long limbs and his fair skin, now turned golden by the hot Grecian sun, conformed more to the Athenian ideal. She said, "I am thinking that Papa should have named you Apollo rather than Ares."

He looked pleased but a little startled by her abrupt change of subject. However, he said, "I am very glad he did not. It has been difficult enough to bear the name of Ares. There were times at Cambridge when it was suggested I ought to live up to it."

She laughed. "It has been suggested by Aunt Caroline and others that it is a pity I do not live up to *my* name. Indeed, I fear I have not always acted with great wisdom." Ruefully she continued, "I wonder how poor Jane is faring."

"I should imagine that she is very happy. But you must not continue to reproach yourself on that count. Even if you'd not lost your temper, I am sure she would have returned to marry Hooks. Furthermore, you seem to be doing well enough without her. I was never in favor of your bringing her— servants are a responsibility and often a liability on a journey such as this. Barnes was longing to come with me, but I decided to be my own valet."

"Jane did not want to come. It was because I begged her that she did." Athena still looked anxious. "That is why I am so concerned about her. I do hope that Mr. Hooks will be kind to her."

"He seems extremely dependable and he loves her to distraction. I could hope that you might do as well when you come to marry."

"I shall not come to marry," she said vehemently.

"Nonsense, you'll change your mind; and let me tell you, my dear Athena, it is time and past time that you stopped wearing the willow for Eames."

"I am not wearing the willow for him," she said scornfully. "He only opened my eye to the perfidy of men."

Laughing, he slipped an arm around her waist. "Child, you've as much notion of men as a new-born kitten. Not all of us are fortune hunters, and you may rest assured that, as your guardian, I shall see to it that you are approached by none other of the breed. I am sure that had I been down from Cambridge when Eames showed face in Aunt Caroline's drawing room, he'd not have dared offer for you." He gave her a loving little squeeze. "You should realize that it's Eames who's the loser. That bit o' muslin he's wed's a grasping little creature who'll waste his patrimony on diamonds. Before he's much older, I fear he'll also discover that, when it comes to virtue, her price is far below rubies. I think he'll be more than aware that he let the real prize slip through his fingers."

Athena laughed derisively. "The prize? I do not believe there are many who share your opinion. If I did not have my inheritance, I doubt that any man would give me more than a passing glance. I am so big and—"

"So beautiful," Ares told her earnestly. "It was well you lost that extra weight, for it has given new contours to your face. Indeed, you look even more like Grandmother's portrait. Papa always insisted you were the very spit of her—I must admit that I did not think the resemblance as marked as he did —but I do now."

"You are my brother," she said fondly.

"And critical," he insisted. "I wish Mama and Papa could see you. I know they'd agree that you've never been in better looks."

"Oh, Ares," she said softly. "You are too kind. I have given you so many problems on this journey."

"You have." He smiled down at her. "But also you've been wretchedly ill. I do not think I've taken that enough into account."

"You shouldn't need to take it into account," she said ashamedly. "I have been horrid. Mama would have been thoroughly disgusted." She gazed at him, adding a little piteously, "I do miss her and Papa . . . they went so quickly. It's not fair. They should have been with us, as they'd planned. They loved Greece so much."

"Do you imagine they are not with us?" he asked her softly. "Can you believe it is only their ashes that we are bringing to Delphi?"

She stared at him in surprise. He was looking out across the waters to the far hills. There was a rapt expression on his face. Her surprise increased. She had never suspected him of harboring a mystical streak. She said, "You are right. I am sure they

53

are with us, in spirit." With a slight shiver, she moved closer to him. In that moment, she had been oddly disturbed. Indeed, it had seemed to her as if a cloud had passed over the sun. However, upon glancing upwards, she found the sun as bright as ever. She had no reason for her little twinge of fear or for the impulse that caused her to say urgently, "You're all I have, Ares, dear. Nothing must ever happen to you."

"To me?" He gave her a tender smile. "To neither of us. I shall make sure of that—for come Yuletide, we are both invited to Clifton-Bastle, did I not tell you?"

"Clifton-Bastle? Sir Harry's estate in Gloucestershire?" she demanded excitely. "No, you did not tell me. Oh, what fun! I do love his horses!"

"And he loves to have you ride them," Ares said meaningfully. "Though I cannot think we shall have much in the way of riding in late December. It always snows very heavily there. Still, I think you should know that he particularly asked that you should be included in the party."

"He didn't!" Athena breathed. "Now you must be teasing me. I am sure that Sir Harry Clifton hardly noticed my existence save as your sister. There were so many pretty females about when we visited him before."

"There might have been, but he did not forget you, at least that was not the impression I had when he proffered the invitation. I ran into him quite by accident at Tattersalls one morning just before we embarked upon this journey. He asked after you and seemed highly elated when I told him it was all off with Eames."

"He had not heard?" she demanded dryly. "I thought all the ton was cognizant of that." A vision of the young baronet arose in her mind. She, her parents and Ares had all been present at his estate. He was handsome—she colored slightly, remembering that he had had a tendency to tease her, but he had also been a bruising rider. One could not but admire his seat on a horse. He had also complimented her for her own prowess in the saddle. They had ridden every morning. She had missed him sadly when she had gone home. She had hoped he might write to her, but he had not. "I was sure he'd forgotten me," she said.

Ares shook his head. "He had a bad fall, he told me. He was laid up for a long time, but he's as good as new now."

"Oh, I do wish I'd known," she said, distressed.

"I expect you might have, if there'd not been all the trouble at home. Harry told me he'd not wanted to intrude upon your grief and then, he'd heard about your betrothal. He does like you, Athena . . . so, my dear, we must both survive until Christmas."

"Oh," she smiled. "We certainly must. Why did you not mention this before?"

"You were so prickly upon the subject of gentlemen."

She looked down. "I do not believe I should have been prickly if you'd told me what Sir Harry said. I did like him—as did Mama, if you recall."

"And Papa, too." Ares put his finger under her chin. "Well, I am glad you are not quite yet a misanthrope. For a while, I was thinking I should not have accepted his invitation."

"I am most pleased that you did." Clasping her arms around his neck, she murmured, "You are really the very best of brothers,

"And you are the loveliest of sisters," he smiled.

"I hope now that you have forgiven me for the advent of Mr. Herriot—admit, my dear, that he is a necessary evil."

"I expect he will be useful once we're ashore. Certainly he was in Malta and Zante."

"And will be doubly so in Greece. Tomorrow morning when we're rested, he'll see that we're given an audience with the Voivode. It seems he knows him."

"The Voivode?" Athena questioned. "What is his function?"

"He's a sort of Lord Mayor, I presume, the reigning Turk in Patras, but answerable to the Pasha of the district. He's a good man, I understand. Enver has some relationship with him; I believe he is a brother to one of his wives. I am not sure of that, though Herriot told me, at least I believe he did."

"You *believe* he did?"

"To tell you the truth, my love, since he has the business so well in hand, I find myself listening to only half of what he says. You know how he's given to explaining and re-explaining matters."

"I know you find it tedious, but you ought to pay attention to him when it comes to such arrangements. Will it be the Voivode who will give us the firmans?"

"Ah, you know about the firmans, then?" He looked at her with some surprise.

"I heard him telling you about them yesterday. They're safe-conduct passes, are they not, admitting us to places which will provide food and shelter?"

He grinned. "If that is what he says they are, then that is how it must be."

"Oh, really, Ares," she began severely. Then her words trailed off as, over her brother's shoulder, she

56

glimpsed Mr. Herriot deep in conversation with Mahmood Enver. The latter was smiling as though well-satisfied. As usual, however, his companion's face was unreadable, but she did not doubt that some manner of transaction was in progress. Even as she watched, Enver turned and looked at her. His smile widening, he favored her with a deep bow.

"Repellent little toad," Ares, who had followed her glance, muttered. " 'Tis said that these Turks are well-regarded by many of our English travelers, but from what I have seen of them . . . that damned fellow's typical of the lot, lounging about the deck, smoking his pipe, counting his beads."

"They say that there are ninety-nine beads and that a good Mohammedan says a prayer a day for each of them. How can anyone think of ninety-nine prayers?" Athena marveled.

"It's a wonder they find time to eat, but Enver seems to have managed." Ares frowned. "Egad, I cannot say that I like the way he's staring at you. For twopence, I'd . . ."

Athena hurriedly put her hand on his arm. "A cat may look at a king without altering the status of either," she hissed warningly. "In a few hours, we shall take leave of him forever. Look instead at . . . ah, Ares!" She turned back toward the mainland. "See, there are orange trees . . . the golden apples of the sun! And the cypress groves . . . Just think, we'll soon be among them in Greece!" Yet, even as she spoke and even as she, together with her brother, admired the hills above the shore with their great orchards of citrus fruit, she was conscious of Enver's beady eyes upon her; and for a reason she did not quite understand, she shuddered. In spite of her excitement over their pending journey, she could almost wish that the requisite months had passed and she, back in England, was riding up the curving, possibly ice-covered carriageway that led to Clifton-Bastle.

Four

As Captain Pappamichaels had predicted, the *Apollo* sailed into the harbor of Patras in the late afternoon. As a gateway to Greece, it was disappointing. Rather than displaying the marble columns of antiquity, the city that sprawled beneath the shadow of Mount Voitha was characterized by the round roofs of mosques built at one time or another during five hundred years of Turkish rule. Still, in the declining light, the slender minarets silhouetted against an orange sky, were singularly felicitous to the eye.

In the crowded harbor, countless tiny boats were to be seen as well as larger vessels flying the flags of a dozen different countries. The quays were filled with people, many of them in the flowing garb of Turks. There was no order among the crowds and those men, entrusted with carrying bales and bundles ashore, were required to fight their way toward the customs houses.

Athena, flanked by her brother and Mr. Herriot, was waiting to be rowed to the mainland. The idea of going into the city had been exciting but was now daunting. It was still very hot and she feared

59

that the masses of citizenry would make their passage through the streets very difficult. Fretfully, she pushed her light silken cloak back over her shoulders, wishing that she had not needed to don it. However, she could not walk through the town in her thin muslin with its low neck and short puffed sleeves. Mr. Herriot, she knew, had not approved of her choice of gown but she could not have worn her gingham traveling ensemble. "I should perish," she had told him indignantly.

Glancing from him to her brother, she could, however, feel sorry for both of them. They were similarly attired in close-fitting buckskin breeches, high leather boots, jackets of superfine cloth, shirts and high muslin cravats. The ancient Greeks with their short, sleeveless tunics had been far wiser, she decided.

"Mademoiselle, I wish you a safe journey."

A heavy, familiar scent of perfume was in her nostrils as she faced Mahmood Enver, who would be the first to leave for the shore. Meeting his heavy-lidded little eyes, she was hard put to answer politely, but she managed to say coldly, "I thank you, sir."

"And you, too, Sir Ares," the Turk pursued. "I pray that our country will live up to all your expectations." Though the sentiments expressed were polite enough, it seemed to Athena that there was an undertone beneath them that confused and worried her.

Ares must have been equally aware of it for his brown gaze was chill and his tone a match for it. "I am sure it will, sir. I thank you."

"Mr. Herriot." Enver bowed again. "As always we are delighted to have you with us. I know that my brother-in-law, the Voivode, shares my sentiments."

"You are very kind, Enver," Mr. Herriot returned. "We shall wait upon him tomorrow."

"I shall inform him of that fact." Enver bowed yet again and moved to the place where the sailors, overseen by his retinue of guards and slaves, were waiting to assist him into the boat.

"I am glad we've finally seen the last of him," Ares muttered.

"I wish it might be the last," Mr. Herriot said. "I imagine, however, that he will be at the Voivode's side tomorrow morning."

"That is unfortunate," Ares grimaced.

"I've no liking for him myself, but since he's well-placed in government here, it's necessary to bear with him."

Thinking of the moment that morning when she had seen Mr. Herriot in conference with the Turk, and recalling the latter's insinuations concerning him, Athena wondered suspiciously if he were being quite frank in his expressed distaste for the man. It was quite possible that Mr. Herriot, with his need for money, had concluded a business arrangement with him. Firming her lips, she decided that if Ares would not heed her, she herself would take care to observe him when he was ostensibly guiding them through those sites where artifacts might be found and acquired.

"Mr. Herriot," Captain Pappamichaels hailed him. "We are ready."

"Good," he called. Turning to Sir Ares, he said urgently, "We will be going ashore now. We must make sure that we keep together. As you can see, there's considerable confusion on the dock and it will be all too easy to become separated." He bent his gaze on Athena. "I must advise you to keep fast hold of your reticule; thievery has been elevated to a fine art here in Patras."

"Naturally, I shall be careful," Athena returned coldly. "I am not without some vestige of intelligence, Mr. Herriot."

His gray gaze flicked over her face. "That is indeed heartening to know, Miss Penrose."

Her eyes widened and she opened her mouth only to close it again on an angry retort. He had been insolent, but she was aware that she had invited it by her untoward response to the counsel it had been his duty to provide. Tossing her head, she fell into step between the two gentlemen and proceeded to the boat.

They had hardly stepped ashore when Athena was forced to agree that Mr. Herriot was indeed, a necessary evil. Thanks to a loud voice, in which he uttered commands in Greek and Turkish, and to the expert use of both elbows, he shepherded his charges through the crowds and onto the street that ran behind the quays with admirable despatch.

As they paused there momentarily, Athena looked about her confusedly. Though their stop in Zante had given her some experience of a Grecian port with its importunate denizens, Patras, being larger, seemed to be peopled with even more of these, all adding a voice to a din which was almost deafening. Everywhere she looked, there was movement and sound. Half-naked, hideously crippled beggars held out thin claw-like hands or, in some instances, the mere stumps of limbs as they screamed for alms; street urchins darted about, laughing shrilly as they snatched bits of fruit or meat from the stalls of irate peddlers, while the air was further rent by the cries of hawkers offering every possible item from the dried tentacles of squid or octopi to worthless charms against malaria. Travelers speaking in scores of different tongues contributed to the babble as they made their way up from the harbor, and often a chorus of complaint arose from pedestrians as some disdainful Turkish official forced his horse among them. Though she never would have admitted it, Athena, pressing close to Ares, was a little frightened; and, glancing up at her brother's face, she found it paling beneath its tan. Mr. Herriot seemed completely unaffected by the turmoil. He might even have found it exhilarating for, with the first smile she had seen on his face, he said reassuringly, "Our lodgings lie at the end of the street." He waved his hand at a thoroughfare stretching before them. "They're not far, not more than a ten-minute walk."

"Is there no carriage that we might hire?" Ares demanded.

"There are few throughout Greece and none here," Mr. Herriot said. "Tomorrow we will procure acceptable mounts, but at present we must rely on our feet. Again, I beg that you will remain as close to me as possible."

It was an injunction with which Athena could now find no quarrel. Her fear was increasing. It was only too apparent to her that there were very few women among the crowds and none dressed as she. She did not welcome the curious glances she received from men, some of whom had the appearance of brigands. In fact, she wished that rather than donning her high-crowned straw bonnet, she might have made use of the all-concealing hood of her cape.

As if he had sensed her trepidation, Mr. Herriot

said, "It is not much further now, Miss Penrose. It is that large white building. You can see it from here. On the left." He pointed.

Looking in the indicated direction, Athena heaved a small sigh of relief. The building was only a few houses away. Then, she started. It seemed to her that out of the corner of her eye, she had seen the plump form of Mahmood Enver, but on turning toward that spot, she did not find him. It was only, she decided, that with their fezzes and their robes, many Turks resembled each other. By now, their erstwhile traveling companion must be relaxing in his seraglio. She made a little face, pitying the hapless wives and concubines who were forced to cater to so unprepossessing a spouse.

They were only a few hundred yards from their quarters when, of a sudden, two men locked in a far from loving embrace, rolled forth from a small café —furiously biting, kicking and pummeling each other and between blows screaming in a villainous-sounding tongue which Athena guessed must be a Grecian dialect, though it was barely understandable. However, their anger needed no translation, and within seconds a large and interested crowd was gathered about them.

"Lord, Lord!" Ares cocked an inquiring eye at the two combatants. "A mill, by Jove." Coming to a stop, he said with a laugh, "Which would have your money, Herriot?" Moving closer to the brawlers, he continued, "I'd lay my blunt on the little—" His words ended abruptly as Mr. Herriot, jumping forward, caught him by the elbow and urgently pulled him back.

"Come away, for God's sake!" he yelled. "There will be a riot and there's no telling . . ."

"Let me go!" Ares glared at him. "I hired you as

my courier not my keeper, Herriot." Wrenching his arm free, Ares strode back to the crowd, which, by this time was beginning to close in on the pair. Many of the bystanders were shouting encouragement and to this babble, Ares defiantly added his voice. Practically in that same instant, a number of belligerent-looking young Turks pushed their way through the crowd to fall upon the fighters, beating them with sticks. With cries of rage, a group of Greeks, who had been idly watching, hurled themselves upon the Turks.

Barely aware of what she was doing, Athena backed off only to feel a hand clamp down on her arm. "Mademoiselle, come, you must not remain here. It is very, very dangerous. You come with me. I will protect you."

Incredulously, she swiveled about to find Mahmood Enver at her side, his hand still locked on her arm in a grasp that was proving unexpectedly powerful. "Please!" She tried to break from his clutch but to no avail. Inexorably, he was dragging her back; and over his shoulder she saw a curtained palanquin several feet away. "Let me go!" she cried sharply, making another futile effort to free herself.

"No, no, no." He shook his head. "You are better with me, my beautiful one. I will take you to a place where you will be safe."

"I do not want to go with you!" she cried hotly. "Ares! Ares!" With another desperate wrench, she managed to twist away from her captor. Running forward to the place where Mr. Herriot and her brother had been standing, she looked for them in vain. They had disappeared into the angry mob. Then, taking another step forward she caught sight of her brother's tall body. He was in the very midst of the struggle. "Ares, Ares, Ares!" she shrieked. To her horror, she saw a staff descend upon his head. He staggered back, fell and was lost to view. "Ares!" She flung herself against those in front of her, only to be seized and yanked back.

"Mademoiselle," Enver panted. "No one can help your brother or Mr. Herriot. Regardez!" He pointed and to her further horror, she saw a contingent of Turkish soldiers wielding the incredibly sharp and curving knives which Mr Herriot had told her were called yataghans. Plunging into the fray, they laid about them ferociously, killing and maiming until the street was slippery with blood.

"No, no, no!" Athena screamed. "Ares ... my brother, Ares!" Enver's arms were tight about her waist, the smell of his perfume was almost suffocating her; worse yet, he had pinioned her arms behind her and, though she continued to struggle, she could not free herself. Then she felt a sharp blow beneath her chin and amidst a startling shower of bright, multi-colored lights which seemed to be behind rather than before her eyes, she fell into blackness.

Athena awakened to the sound of voices, men's voices, not far away. Dazedly, she listened, straining to distinguish words, wondering where she was and when she had fallen asleep. She had dreamed of ... of ... or had it been a dream—the screams, the yelling? She moved her fingers and felt material beneath them, rough, ridged material ... a carpet? No, for there was softness under her, too. She tried to lift her head; it felt heavy and it ached. Her chin ached, too. Then, with a little hissing gasp, she remembered the fighting in the streets, the fighting that had happened so suddenly and *Ares*—Ares being struck down and she unable to run to his aid. Something had caught her—someone . . . Enver—Mahmood Enver . . . Sights, sounds, pain and her hands pinioned behind her back. She remembered more. She had tried to get away from him and he had struck her. Memory faded after the blow... and now, the softness below her and the continuing murmur. She opened her eyes to dimness, to a wall on which a latticed shadow danced, a round, swaying latticed shadow. Her gaze flickered away from it. There was a low table beside whatever she was lying upon. The table was covered with metal—she knew that because it had a dull sheen. There was a tall, curving jug on it. It, too, seemed to be fashioned from metal. Its spout was thin, and so was its handle. Looking up, she saw an archway and beyond that... blackness. The blackness disturbed her. There was an odd, pungent smell in her nostrils which was even more disturbing. It was not familiar, nothing was familiar... but Ares, what had happened to Ares? That was what mattered—that was all that mattered. "Ares, Ares, Ares..." she moaned, trying to sit up only to feel weak and dizzy... and where was she? With Enver?

The voices had ceased abruptly. Someone was kneeling beside her. A hand was placed beneath her head and at her lips was metal. "Open, please, Mees." The person with the hand must be speaking. It was a man who had spoken in heavily accented English. "Come, drink, Mees."

"Enver?" She tried to turn her head but she could not move it—he was holding it and forcing her lips apart with the metal neck of a bottle; there was a fiery liquid in her mouth. She swallowed convulsively, choked and coughed. More liquid seeped into her mouth, sliding down her throat. She did not feel the worse for it. It seemed to make everything inside her head much clearer. The man beside her was still shadowy, though. She saw that he had a beard. He was not Enver; he was bigger than Enver. A little thrill of fear shot through her. Was he a servant of the Turk? And where was she? Panic threaded her tone as she demanded, "Where did he take me? You have no right . . . I . . ."

"Miss Penrose, please, you must not be afraid."

She started, recognizing that voice, recognizing its ring of authority, even though it was muted. "Mr. H-Herriot!" She turned her head but saw only the man beside her, who was not Mr. Herriot. "Where . . ." she began.

Mr. Herriot spoke again from somewhere in the room, "Allow me to present to you Dr. Megasthenes."

She barely heard the introduction. Her fear had increased. She was remembering, remembering Mr. Herriot and Enver deep in conversation. "Why have you done this?" she accused. "You and Enver . . . why?"

"Enver?" he repeated wonderingly.

"Enver?" boomed Dr. Megasthenes. He arose. He was very tall and dressed in a long loose gown.

"I do not think she is fully conscious yet," Mr. Herriot said. "She hit her head when he knocked her down."

"No," she protested. "I do remember now. You were talking with him . . . about the statues, I thought, but you must have been planning . . . *this*. How much did he pay you?"

"She is delirious," the doctor said positively.

"No, I am not," she asserted. "He and Enver . . . they plotted. . ."

"Miss Penrose," Mr. Herriot said curtly, "you are mistaken."

"Yes, most strangely mistaken," the doctor corroborated. "If it were not for my dear friend, Sable—"

"You need not defend me, Dimitri," Mr. Herriot told him abruptly. "I need no defense. Obviously, Miss Penrose is confused. I cannot think it surprising. She has passed through a harrowing experience, and her brother . . ."

"My brother!" Athena struggled to a sitting position, finding that the latticed shadow had been cast by an ornamental brass globe in which a candle flickered. She was in a rug-hung room with low ceilings and furnished with several divans. There was movement to the left of her and looking in that direction, she saw Mr. Herriot. "Oh," she gasped. He, too, had been hurt, possibly badly. A blood-stained bandage encircled his head, one eye was swollen shut, his lips were bruised and, glancing down, she found that there were streaks of blood on his shirt. "Good God, what happened!" she cried.

"It does not matter," he shrugged.

"That is not true," the doctor contradicted. "She should know, Sable, that you were almost killed by this man with whom you were supposedly making these fine plans. If you will not tell her what you may have brought upon yourself by—"

Mr Herriot stiffened, "Please, Dimitri," he began in a low voice.

"I will not. She must . . ."

"Hsst." Mr. Herriot laid his hand on Dr. Megasthenes's sleeve. "Outside . . ."

The doctor was silent, his head cocked in a listening position. "Yes," he whispered. "I hear." He fell silent.

The tension in the room was almost tangible, Athena thought, looking at them wonderingly. She started as she heard a tentative knock. Glancing at the archway, she perceived a door, but neither man made a move in its direction. Again there was a knock and after a slight pause, three more knocks were heard, one following the other in rapid succession.

"Ah," Dr. Megasthenes expelled a deep breath. "It is Vasillos. You remain here," he cautioned as he strode into the archway.

Obeying his friend's instructions, Mr. Herriot remained where he was, frowning into the darkness. The sound of a chain rattling and then of a bolt being drawn back reached Athena's ears. Immediately afterwards, a gust of warm air smote her in the face. There was an almost inaudible murmur and then the door was shut and bolted again. Dr. Megasthenes came slowly back into the room, looking gravely at Mr. Herriot. Speaking in his native Greek, he said, "It is as you feared, Sable. The wound was of the flesh—he survives and he is conscious. Also, he demands vengeance. Already they have gone to the lodging house and to the home of your consul, which is now under surveillance. A watch has been posted at the quays and with the first rays of the sun, there will be a house-to-house search."

"I feared as much," Mr. Herriot said grimly. "His attendants intervened . . . but no matter, we've not the time to repine over that. We must go and soon. I cannot think that Miss Penrose could appeal . . ."

"She could appeal to no one," Dr. Megasthenes said quickly. "If she is discovered . . . it will be Enver."

"She must not be discovered," Mr. Herriot

rasped. "Yet, I cannot think that she will be able to walk so far. She is gently bred, unused to hardship and in pain."

"I am not in pain," Athena stated. "What do you want of me? What has happened?"

Both men looked at her in surprise. "The young lady speaks our tongue!" Dr. Megasthenes exclaimed.

"So I was told," Mr. Herriot said, "but I did not realize how well."

"Dr. Megasthenes spoke about houses being searched," Athena continued, "and you've not yet explained about Enver . . ."

Mr. Herriot's mouth twisted. "You had your own explanations, Miss Penrose."

"Enough!" ordered Dr. Megasthenes. Breaking into Greek again, he spoke quickly, urgently but, to Athena, almost incomprehensibly.

"Please." She raised her hand. "I can catch only a few words. Enver is wounded and you, Mr. Herriot, had something to do with it . . ?"

"That is the way of it, Miss Penrose. When Sir Ares—"

"Ares!" she cried, "Oh my God, I saw him fall. . . ."

Mr. Herriot said heavily, "You must believe that I tried desperately to reach him, but he was in the thick of the fray and I could not."

There was a painful pounding in Athena's throat. It was hard for her to speak over it. "He . . . he's not . . ." She could not bring herself to complete the awful question.

"I cannot tell you. I, too, saw him fall."

"Struck down," she moaned. "And those dreadful men with their knives . . ."

"Yes, but still they might not have touched him. He had already fallen; he may only have lost consciousness and suffered a few contusions. But, again, I can tell you nothing for I saw you attempting to go to him and Enver behind you. I knew I had to stop him."

"How severely did you wound him?" she asked in a small shamed voice.

"Not severely enough. I wanted to kill him. I wish I had. You see, he knows that it was I who was his assailant and he will complain to his brother-in-law. Enver is a most influential and vindictive man and I am sure his fury knows no bounds. I gave him an injury which has incapacitated him for life. He will do his utmost to hunt us down. Soldiers will be dispatched."

"To search the houses," she said. "That is why it is necessary to leave before dawn."

"It is our only chance and a slim one. We'd need to go on foot and in disguise, for there will be many watching for us and the governors of other districts alerted. Unfortunately, Enver knows you were going to Delphi, so we dare not take that route. Our only hope is to make our way to Athens. There I have many friends among the Turkish officials— they will listen and protect us. But it will be a dangerous journey from the beginning, for we must needs cross the mountains."

"In the dark?"

He shook his head. "No, there's a cave that Dimitri knows of in the foothills. We will rest there until daybreak and then be on our way. Our pursuers will not believe that we have dared to leave the city after nightfall, so we will have an advantage. Another advantage is my own knowledge of the territory. I have tramped all through these mountains." He gave her a grim look. "As I have said, it is a very slim chance, but if we remain here . . ."

"No," she said. "I agree that we dare not remain here. But Ares . . ."

"Dimitri will try and find him. Since he is a doctor, he has many connections in Patras among the Turks as well as the Greeks. Neither you nor I would be of any help to your brother now." He regarded her doubtfully. "But I wonder if you can endure the hardships that will inevitably be our lot?"

Her heart was pounding even harder. Grief for Ares was intermingled with panic. Mr. Herriot was eyeing her warily. She could not blame him. He had seen her at her very worst and she was well aware that in offering to take her with him, he must believe that he was severely endangering his own chance for survival. He could not hanker for her company; nor, for that matter, did she for his, but the alternative was far worse. She said crisply, "I am strong and healthy, Mr. Herriot, and I do not fear hardship, but what of you? You've been hurt. Your head, your eye . . ."

Mr. Herriot's battered lips twitched into a brief smile." I do not walk with my head or my eye, and my feet are well able to bear me wherever I choose to go."

"As are mine," she stated. She rose. "I am used to walking for miles at home and I do not tire easily. When must we be ready?"

"In an hour's time."

She drew a deep breath. "Good. I am sure that the sooner we go, the better it will be for us. You talked about disguises?"

Dr. Megasthenes said, "I shall see to that. I know where I can procure feminine attire."

"And none to ask questions?" Mr. Herriot demanded edgily.

"I have but to say that you have wounded Enver, and there will be no questions." The doctor's eyes glinted.

"Oh," Athena gasped. As the two men stared at her, she continued, "The urns . . . my parents' ashes are in our luggage, which must yet be aboard the *Apollo*. What will happen to them?"

"Word has been sent to Pappamichaels. Your luggage will be sent with mine to Athens . . . to the house of Eustacia Palomides, who is a friend of mine," Mr. Herriot explained.

Tears stood in Athena's eyes but she blinked them back. The recent events had almost made her forget the reason that had brought her brother and herself to Greece. It was, she thought dolefully, all too possible that more than the ashes of her parents would find a haven in that honored earth.

Five

The three-quarter moon had seemed remarkably bright when they had emerged from the doctor's house, but now Athena, following the doctor's dark bulk up a narrow winding street, could barely see him. The eaves of the houses on either side of them projected out so far that they formed an arch that shut out all view of the sky. It felt as if the air had been similarly closed off. It was still very warm and an amalgam of unappetizing smells rose from the filthy ground; more than once, she had stepped into substances of a nature she preferred not to ascertain. She was glad of her stout shoes and heavy cotton stockings. They had been rough to her feet and they were not a perfect fit, but at least they offered protection from the stony soil. Her garments were equally protective, she thought with some satisfaction. They consisted of two petticoats, a long and full blue skirt, a white, tunic-like blouse, a short blue singlet and a red sash which she wore loosely knotted about her waist. Though the material was a heavy homespun, it was proving oddly comfortable for, aside from the drawstring of her skirt, there was nothing to bind her, no corselet to wear, no small pesky buttons to fasten. She liked the scarf that the doctor had showed her how to wind about her head, turban-fashion. It was light and unlike her bonnet, it did not scratch the back of her neck. Though the rough, dark cloak she wore was too warm, she knew she would need it both for concealment and as a blanket. There was only one item that gave her pause, the wide brass band encircling the third finger of her left hand. According to Dr. Megasthenes, it was an absolute necessity to establish the appearance of a matrimonial relationship with her companion. "Else you would be open to slights, sneers and worse. Sable cannot always be with you."

In spite of this sound reasoning, it had taken both his and Mr. Herriot's earnest persuasions before she would consent to wear it. "Could I not be your sister?" she had pleaded. "We are both dark."

"I fear not, Miss Penrose." Mr. Herriot had given her a wry smile. "There might be many who'd court my sister but none, I hope, would dare make free with my wife."

His expression had informed her that he was no more anxious than she to pretend to a relationship which was, she was sure, as repugnant to him as it was to her. Inadvertently, she touched the ring and found the metal cool against her fingertips. At least she could be sure that he would not presume upon the fictitious relationship!

She cast a look back over her shoulder and was slightly startled. Whenever she thought of Mr. Herriot, she always imagined his tall, elegant figure. However, he, like herself, was clad in rough, shapeless garments. His trousers, after the custom of the country, where almost as full as her skirts and were topped by a loose jacket and a shirt open at the collar. He, too, wore a turban-like covering on his head, which was as well, for it hid his fashionably coiffed hair. He had also, though very reluctantly, promised Dimitri not to shave. She recalled his rueful comment, "I vow I'd not do it except to save my life, for I've always had a dislike for facial hair. No offense intended, Dimitri."

The bearded doctor had laughed, "None taken, my friend." Sobering; he had added meaningfully, "You remember that it is to save your life. And I charge you, Sable, there is much fever about this summer, especially where there are stagnant pools and swampy marshes. If either of you become ill, do not allow anyone to bleed you. It only weakens the body and at the same time strengthens the hold of the pestilence."

"You forget that I have some knowledge of medicine myself, Dimitri."

"Ah, that is true enough!" The doctor's rumbling laugh had resounded through the room again. "I was forgetting it. I must be growing old, for it was that which brought us together, five years back, when you were accompanying young Ingram to the Morea. Yes, you are uncommonly knowledgeable for a layman and I am glad of it, for it would be unwise to seek the aid of any of those Grecian quacks that proliferate like ants in villages and are about as useful. The Turks, in general, are fine physicians, but, of course, they keep their knowledge for their own. I should not be surprised if they were trying to kill the Greeks that way—but enough, I'll not waste your precious time in talking about one sickness for which we have yet no cure."

Athena frowned. She was remembering Mr. Herriot's injuries, and notwithstanding his boasts concerning his medical knowledge, it seemed to her that their projected journey might be very difficult for him. The doctor had also expressed concern but

77

Herriot had only shrugged and replied nonchalantly, "These are but superficial scratches. They trouble me less than the bites of a mosquito." As if to emphasize his meaning, he had immediately shouldered the large pack Dr. Megasthenes had prepared and disdained any help in strapping it to his back. She did not believe herself wrong in attributing this gesture to pride. Not too long ago, she had made a similar gesture as she stood in the prow of *The Scorpion* as it headed toward the open sea. She hoped devoutly that Mr. Herriot would not, like herself, have reason to regret his display of bravado.

"Sssss." Dr. Megasthenes's hiss was hardly louder than a breath, but it reached her ears and behind her Mr. Herriot also halted. The sound of her own breathing frightened her. It seemed too loud in the silence. She drew a breath in and held it. Somewhere in the nearly Stygian darkness ahead there was the sound of footsteps. Were they proceeding toward them? It was impossible to tell.

She bit down an exclamation—she had heard a scuffling noise. It was followed by a cry that was quickly muted into a choking gurgle. There was no doubt that the footsteps were diminishing. She found that she was cold, yet beads of perspiration were fast turning into rivulets that trickled down her body. The thought of the death that had taken place a few paces ahead of her made her long to scream. She clamped her teeth together, thrusting her tongue against the backs of them, swallowing spasmodically. For the first time in her life she fully understood what was meant by the "taste of fear."

Dr. Megasthenes moved ahead. Athena followed. When she thought that she could no longer bear the stench and the heat of the noisome alleys, they emerged into the open. She had a glimpse of a starry sky and moon-edged waters, but kept her eyes on the path, faintly visible in the moonlight. It was narrow and ran between tall dry grasses; burrs scratched her legs through her stockings. The hill was steep; it was hard going. Her breath came in gasps—then finally, they were close to the top.

"Stop," Dr. Megasthenes whispered.

They halted.

"You must come this way," he told Athena. "Take my hand and place one foot after the other in a straight line. I will show you." Striking a flint, he held the flame downwards, illuminating a narrow path bordered on one side by a rocky cliff. She did not see a cave cut into its rugged face, but trustingly, she edged after him. A few minutes later, he stopped again. He dropped her hand, produced a small lantern, and lit it. "It is here."

Holding up the lantern, he indicated a crevice. It seemed very narrow but a close glance showed her that it could easily accommodate them. She slipped inside, into total darkness which, to her relief, was vanquished by the small lantern. Dr. Megasthenes slid in after her.

A second later, Mr. Herriot followed her. Dr. Megasthenes motioned him to remain by the mouth of the cave, and spoke to him in a low voice. She could not hear him. Probably she was not meant to hear. It did not matter. She was too weary to be curious; she only wanted somewhere to rest. A few feet away, she saw a clearing backed by large boulders. Near them, a pile of old woolen blankets suggested that the cave had often been used as a hiding place.

"Child." Dr. Megasthenes came to her side. Grasping her hands, he whispered, "Unfortunately,

I must return immediately—there is a patient who comes late. If I am gone, unfortunate questions will be asked. I wish you a safe journey and I beg you will be patient with Sable. You are in good hands. Trust him and, if he needs help, I pray you will give it. May God be with you." Without waiting for her answer, he was gone.

A muttered exclamation drew her attention to Mr. Herriot, who stood just inside the cave. He was fumbling with the straps of the pack. He appeared to be having some difficulty with the buckles.

"Let me do that," she said, half expecting a protest; but he said nothing. He only stood waiting while she unbuckled it. Then he started to help her ease it to the ground; but in the midst of that action, he sighed and sagged against her. He had fainted! She caught him in her arms and lowered him carefully to the floor of the cave. She was about to drag him to the blankets but changed her mind. She did not know how long they had lain there or to what purpose they had been put. They might be very dirty. Quickly she took off her cloak and slid it beneath him. He was so inert that she was frightened. Picking up the lantern, she directed its wavering flame toward his face. He was very pale; he seemed scarcely to be breathing. She knelt beside him and placed her hand in the region of his heart. It was beating strongly but she felt a sticky moisture on his shirt. She held the lantern closer and saw a large patch of blood. Quickly she set the lantern down, pulled back his jacket and opened his shirt, gasping as she saw a blood-soaked bandage wrapped around his ribs. Momentarily, she was terrified but it was not the time to consider her emotions. He needed all her attention. She remembered that she had put the contents of her reticule into a secret and capacious pocket in her petticoat. Among them was a small scissors. She took it out and cut the bandage away. Again she was frightened of what she might find; and certainly the wound, smeared with blood, was not pretty. Not far from the heart, it was a gash that ran the length of four ribs; she guessed that he had been slashed by one of those murderous yataghans. Further examination told her that the cut had been glancing for it was not overly deep. Still, it must have been very painful and to have walked such a distance with a pack weighing him down had been the height of folly! She wondered that the doctor had sanctioned it when she might easily have borne part of the burden. Then, she realized that, given Mr. Herriot's obstinacy and determination, argument would have been futile. It also occurred to her that Dr. Megasthenes must have been well aware of Mr. Herriot's plight, hence his parting words. She was sure, too, that the doctor would have included materials for bandaging in the contents of the pack.

She moved to the bundle and turned it over, frowning at its bulk and weight. Upon opening it, she found several flasks, a wooden water canteen, a parcel of food and cups. There was also a thin wool blanket and changes of garments for them both—and all this a wounded man had carried up the steep incline to the cave! That climb would have been bad enough in itself, but they had walked at least three miles before reaching the foothills. Sighing, she hunted for the bandages and found several rolls of linen. She opened the canteen and poured some of the water onto a piece of linen. She managed to take off his shirt, inadvertently noticing his well-muscled arms and wide chest tapering to a narrow waist—his proportions were not unlike those of a

Greek statue she had seen at the British museum. She blushed and hurriedly washed the wound. She unrolled more linen, cut off a piece and folded it several times, then placed it against the cut and wrapped the rest of the bandage around his waist, tying it tightly. Then she took out the extra shirt in the pack and put it on him.

During these ministrations, Athena had been glad that he had remained unconscious. However, once she had completed them, she was disturbed, wondering how she might revive him. She had no smelling salts. Burnt feathers were known to help, but she had no feathers either. Pouring water over his face might suffice. She was about to fetch the canteen when she heard a long sigh that ended in a groan. Hastily, she bent over him. His lashes were fluttering—she had not realized how long they were. He opened his good eye and looked at her dazedly. "I must . . . I . . ." He frowned confusedly.

"You fainted."

"Fainted?" he repeated uncomprehendingly. There was an edge of anger to his voice as he questioned, "I—fainted?"

"Or fell unconscious—I believe they are one and the same thing. The slash on your ribs must have caused you a good deal of pain. It was also bleeding, which I presume you knew. Why did you not tell the doctor? He might have tended it."

"He had to get back . . . and I thought it was nothing." He tried to shrug and winced.

"Nothing!" She glared at him. "When we are running for our lives? How dare you take on the burden of that heavy pack in your condition? You were not only endangering yourself, you were endangering both of us. It was very foolish!"

A dark flush mounted to his cheeks. "What

could I do?" he retorted defensively. "You could not have shouldered it."

"Not all of it," she allowed, "but I could have shared the weight of it. I am no fragile flower, Mr. Herriot. I am tall and strong. But enough." She continued in a softer tone. "Are you feeling more the thing?"

"Yes . . . quite." He pressed his hand to his side, then regarded her in surprise. "The bandage is dry."

"I changed it, and your shirt, too. The others were soaked with blood." Concernedly, she added, "I hope I did not tie the bandage too tightly."

Again he flushed darkly, "It . . . it was quite unnecessary for you to have tended me. I could have—"

"Come," she broke in impatiently, "I have some knowledge of wounds. Two years ago my horse, Sebastian, tore his side on a nail. I did not like the way my groom was caring for him, so I treated him myself. Now, would you have wine? Dr. Megasthenes has given us several flasks."

"No," he said quickly. "I want only to . . . rest a bit." Then, as if fearing she might believe he was showing an unmanly weakness, he told her authoritatively, "We must both rest, for, as you know, we must be up before dawn."

"I am not at all sure that you ought to—" she began.

"Nonsense," he interrupted acerbically, "I am only tired. It has been rather . . . a long day . . ." His voice faltered, trailing away into a weary sigh, and his eye closed.

For a moment she feared he had fainted a second time, but on bending over him and seeing the steady rising and fall of his chest, she guessed that he had merely fallen asleep.

As she tiptoed away from him, she glanced toward the pile of blankets behind her, wondering if she should rest on them but, when she examined them more closely, she found that, as she had feared, they were dirty and smelled strongly of goat. She remembered the blanket in the pack, but it was wrapped around other items and the idea of taking them out was suddenly more than she could face. All she really wanted to do was sleep. Choosing a spot a few feet away from Mr. Herriot, she sank down. She had never lain on so hard a surface. She hoped that she would be able to sleep but that, she feared, was doubtful. Yet, if they were to rise so early, she must make the effort. She must . . .

A hand was on her shoulder, shaking it gently. "Jane" Athena demanded crossly. "Why are you waking me so soon . . . you . . ." She paused; memory had returned. She sat up immediately to find Mr. Herriot, jacket on, standing over her. "Oh," she regarded him with some concern. "Should you be up? Your side . . ."

"Is much better," he finished with a touch of hauteur. "I am not a fragile flower, either, Miss Penrose. Indeed, I am a very hardy plant!" He paused and then said almost reluctantly, "But I cannot help but think that your groom's neglect was a most fortunate circumstance for me. Still—" and here he frowned—"you should not have put your cloak beneath me and slept on this hard ground. Here are blankets . . ." he gestured at the pile.

"They are filthy and reek of goat." She wrinkled her nose.

"All the same, I could have borne with them. It was not necessary that you—"

"Mr. Herriot," she broke in. "It was extremely necessary for my own preservation. I am dependent upon you. Consequently, you must not become incapacitated."

There was a slight twitch at the corners of his mouth. "There's not the slightest danger of my becoming incapacitated. However, I am thinking that an impartial observer might have some difficulty in deciding which of us has been the more dependent, Miss Penrose."

In spite of that faint smile, she detected a rueful note in his voice and guessed that he must still be bitterly regretting his moment of weakness. She said quickly, "He would know that it was I." She flushed, suddenly prodded by memory. "If it had not been for your intervention yesterday..." She shuddered and looked away from him.

"Miss Penrose." His tone was unexpectedly gentle. "Let us not speak of yesterday."

She kept her head down, eyes on a small insect that was traversing a strip of ground illumined by the flame of the lantern. "I have not asked your pardon for suggesting that you and Enver..." there was a lump in her throat and tears were threatening. "And you so h-hurt h-helping me. I do not understand how I came to imagine that..." She did sob then.

"Come." He knelt beside her. "It does not matter. You were confused." He put his hand on her shoulder and gave it a tiny shake. "Furthermore, if you continue to waste time in these fruitless recriminations, we'll be the later in starting, and that, I need not tell you, would hardly be advisable."

"Oh." She faced him. "I am sorry."

He rose and went back to the pack. "You must eat something. There's feta, black olives, bread and wine. You might find the cheese, the olives and the wine a little strange-tasting at first—the Greeks put resin in their wine—but I think you will not think it unpalatable. However, even if you do, you ought to eat a goodly portion; we have a long walk ahead of us."

"A walk in which we will share the burden of the pack," she said firmly.

"I assure you that I am quite myself this morning and—"

"If we do not share it, I shall not stir a step from this cave. The doctor has said that the way is steep and if you should become faint and fall, what would I do?"

"Miss Penrose," Mr. Herriot said gravely, "I have the notion that you would do very well, indeed; but since I must think of you as my employer, I have no choice but to acquiesce."

Six

The sun had been up for over three hours and though it was far from its zenith, the air was very warm and heavy with moisture. Athena, trudging behind Mr. Herriot, could see the distant band of white-blue water which was the gulf. Impossible to believe that they had sailed into it only a day and a half earlier, she and Ares, excited and eager to set foot upon the fabled soil of Greece. Resolutely, she swallowed a lump in her throat as there rose unbidden in her mind a vivid image of her last glimpse of him—felled by a blow from a stave, while about him ferocious Turkish soldiers wielded knives, indifferent as to whom they wounded. Another image replaced the first—Mr. Herriot's slashed body. She winced. A little deeper . . . but it had not been deeper. That did not make it any the less painful; and despite that pain, it must have been he who had borne her to Dr. Megasthenes's house, where she had awakened full of unfounded accusations. She sighed. Off and on during the morning, she had wondered how she had ever come to credit Mahmood Enver's statements; she had loathed him from the moment she had first laid eyes on him. Yet there was no reason to hide the truth from herself. Her ready belief was based on her dislike for the man who had saved her from the Turk, and in so doing had placed himself in the greatest jeopardy.

She cast a nervous glance over her shoulder, but she saw no more than she had been seeing since they had emerged from the cave, a tangle of shrubbery and stunted trees below great black crags seamed with fissures, their surfaces glinting like diamonds whenever they were hit by the sun's rays. The path they were following brought them close to these rocky projections, necessitating that they move with great caution, and keep constantly on the lookout for loose stones on which they could slide or trip. Yet, as Mr. Herriot had instructed, it was better to remain as close to that side of the trail as possible; for, more than once, they had passed areas where the way was horridly narrow and to look down was to see deep ravines filled with jagged boulders. If she were awed by the landscape, it also had the effect of minimizing her earlier fears. When she had followed Mr. Herriot from the cave, the wrath of Mahmood Enver was large in her mind and she could imagine a contingent of fierce Turkish soldiers, like those she had seen patrolling the quays of Zante and the streets of Patras, stealthily climbing up the mountains, inexorably pursuing them. Now she thought it well-nigh impossible that anyone could search them out in this vast and almost impenetrable terrain. Rather than continuing at this relatively fast pace, it seemed to her that they might have taken their time, but Mr. Herriot evidently disagreed. He went doggedly onward, stopping only to help her over boulder-strewn gullies or places where the grass grew thick and tangled. She had protested at one juncture, explaining that she was used to walking and climbing. "I cannot think that this is much worse than roaming through the Scottish Highlands, and I have spent many summers among those peaks."

She smiled ruefully in recollection. Beyond cautioning her not to talk so loudly, he had ignored her assurances and stubbornly continued to offer a hand whenever he deemed it necessary. Obviously he was not a man to whom one could dictate. She had a feeling that he had been born to command and wondered what his background was. Certainly, he was of gentle birth and Ares had told her that Sir Edwin Calthrope knew his family and thought highly of him—but beyond confiding this information to her brother, Sir Edwin had said nothing more. That, Ares, contended, probably meant that Mr. Herriot, in common with other young sprigs of the nobility, had run up huge gambling debts and, in consequence, had been disinherited. "A bit of a loose screw, I think."

At the time, she had been more than willing to accept this conclusion, but no longer. A "loose screw" signified a man of little character. Such an individual would not have taken his responsibilities so seriously—responsibilities he had not sought but which had been thrust upon him by that ridiculous bet. He had not wanted to come with them. He had also told Ares that a woman had no place on a journey such as he contemplated. Yet, once they had embarked upon it, he had been of inestimable help and even though he disliked and probably despised her, he had risked his life to save her. Now he was in even greater danger and less able to cope with it. She was worried about him. More than once, his steps had seemed to lag and his shoulders had drooped. Then he had straightened up and strode on, moving even faster than before.

The words he had spoken at Dr. Megasthenes's house came back to her: "I do not walk with my head or my eye, Miss Penrose." If he had made that statement at this present moment, she would have retorted, "No, you walk with your *will*, and you ought not to tax your strength in this manner." She wished she had the courage to make that comment. Despite his assurances that he was used to hardship, it could not be easy trudging a path that was proving to be all uphill. However, the summit was not very far ahead; he had almost reached it.

Then he suddenly halted, pressing back against the cliff and staring down. She was about to ask what he saw; but, even as she opened her mouth on the question, he turned toward her, frowning and pressing a finger to his lips and with the other hand motioning to her to hurry. Once she had reached him, he pointed. Looking in that direction, she froze. A small contingent of Turkish soldiers was seen winding up the mountain. Although they must have started much later than the two they evidently pursued, they were not as far off as might have been expected. The reason for that was immediately observable: they were walking carefully but also surely and quickly. Obviously, they had been over that trail many times. Athena clutched Mr. Herriot's arm and whispered, "What .. ?"

"We must go on. There will be a cave or a tree. I shall find a place to hide us. Never fear, we will be safe."

He had spoken as positively as usual, but she was not convinced of the safety he promised. If they could find a cave or a tree, their pursuers could also find it and rout them out. Then ... But she dared not contemplate what might happen then.

"Come," he ordered brusquely.

In a moment they had gained the summit of the trail. But rather than descending immediately, Mr. Herriot came to another stop. He was frowning and Athena, staring at the path, swallowed bubbles of fear. It was almost perpendicular; worse yet, it was covered with dry grass and strewn with small rocks. They were in danger of slipping and sliding, and to their left yawned a gorge which looked to be a thousand feet deep.

He seized her arm and whispered, "Stay close to this side." Pointing to the rocks, he continued, "Hold onto these and crouch down as I do." Half-kneeling, he started downwards, holding on to the rock-faced cliff. She followed him. Descending was not as terrifying as it had seemed, but it was slow going, very slow. Then her foot slipped, dislodging a shower of little stones into the gorge; to her horror, she heard them rain down on the rocks below and knew that their pursuers must also have heard and been alerted by the sound.

"I am s—" In her trepidation, she had spoken out loud, but before she could utter another word, he had placed his hand over her mouth, shaking his head.

Flushing, she gave him an apologetic look and nodded.

Finally they reached level ground again. They came through the bushes and emerged into a small clearing surrounded by trees. Through them, she heard the splashing of a waterfall. Mr. Herriot had halted and was staring upwards. On a plateau overhead, she saw a cave. Though it was halfway up an even steeper incline than that which they had just ascended, it did not seem inaccessible. In fact, it might be relatively easy to reach it because there was soil where one could find a foothold and plants to grasp. Impulsively, she started forward, but he caught her arm, whispering, "We must go further. I cannot like ..." His words died on his lips and he whirled around, staring at the trees.

Athena followed his gaze and saw a number of roughly-dressed men emerging. All of them carried muskets and they wore yataghans stuck in heavy leather belts that held one or more pistols; cartridge holders were strapped across their breasts. Mr. Herriot stood very still, and instinctively Athena moved nearer to him. He put an arm around her waist and drew her even closer. Through clenched teeth, he muttered, "Speak as little as possible and only in Greek."

In a trice they were surrounded. There were five of them, all wearing rough, patched shirts and breeches of goatskin. High leather boots covered their legs, and their heads were adorned with battered sheepskin caps. Though their coloring was dissimilar, two being very dark with fierce black eyes while two others were fair and the fifth, red-headed, they had a resemblance that went deeper than feature. There was a ferocity and a wariness about them that reminded Athena of a wolf she had once seen in a London menagerie. Her heart was beating so heavily that she feared the sound must be audible. Without doubt, she knew that she was seeing some of the notorious bandits that were said to infest the mountains, preying on travelers.

The red-headed man stepped forward. He was very tall with a powerful frame and heavy muscles. He stared at Mr. Herriot and grinned revealing a mouth full of jagged, rotting teeth. His clothing was filthy; his skin, too, was encrusted with dirt. Looking at his hands, Athena had great difficulty in restraining a shudder; his nails were long, black and curved like talons. So fetid was the odor that arose from him that she wished she might only breathe out and not in. In a hoarse, ugly voice, he said in Greek, "Good morning, my friend, and where might you be bound?"

Mr. Herriot said in one deep breath, "My wife and I are bound to Koto . . . to visit her parents." To her amazement, Athena heard a distinct quaver in his tone.

"Indeed?" the man returned. "Whence have you come, friend?"

"From P-Patras, your worship." The quaver in Mr. Herriot's voice was more pronounced.

"From Patras, eh? A seaport town. No doubt you are bringing many fine gifts to your relations."

"N-No, your w-worship," Mr. Herriot stuttered. "We are p-poor people . . . we have a . . . a f-few food stuffs with us. No more. I . . . I swear it, your w-worship."

The man grinned and winked at one of the other men, who promptly gave a great guffaw. "Kostas, here, is inclined not to believe you, nor am I. Kostas thinks you'd not have set out on your travels to Koto without some coins to pay your way." His laugh turned into a snarl. "Isn't that the truth of it, my friend?"

"W-We are poor p-people, your worship," Mr. Herriot repeated giving him a terrified look. "There . . . there is little chance for a man such as myself t-to earn much money, not with the T-Turks about . . ."

The bandit winked again. "Ah, it goes ill with us Greeks in this tortured land. We are all poor and must eke out our living in ways that might not please everyone, but live we must, eh, my friend from Patras?"

"Y-Yes, your worship, I...I am glad your w-worship understands that. All of us p-poor Greeks of this once great country are...are ground beneath the heel of the T-Turkish oppressor and... and...and being G-Greeks, t-together, should r-remember that."

Throwing back his great head, the bandit laughed loudly, the sound of that laughter being quickly caught by an echo and eerily repeated in the distance. Then with a glare of contempt, he caught Mr. Herriot by the ear, and twisted it cruelly, and said loudly over his victim's agonized howl, "Would you think to gain my sympathy, friend? Kyriakos Andrutzos claims no kinship with a yellow-livered coward such as you."

He barked a command at his followers, and in seconds the men had relieved Mr. Herriot and Athena of their bundles. The brigands tossed them on the ground and opened them. The flasks of wine and the cheese they stuffed quickly into their shirts. Then, searching through the packs, they took out the clothing. When one held up Athena's extra petticoat, she felt Mr. Herriot stiffen. She wondered why he should be so concerned over a mere petticoat, but when she met the eyes of the man who had appropriated it, she bit down a moan of fear. There was something menacing, something terrible about his expression. Still staring at her, he nudged the man next to him and he, too, looked at her, his eyes slowly going the length of her whole body. She pressed closer to Mr. Herriot and felt his arm tighten convulsively around her.

"Well." Andrutzos moved closer to Mr. Herriot. "You've afforded us food and drink. Now, my friend, empty your pockets."

94

Mr. Herriot cringed. "W-would you take all we have, your worship? We . . . we have a long journey ahead of us . . . and without f-food and m-money, what may we d-do?"

"As to that, my friend, your journey might not be as long as you believe if you do not produce what you have in your pockets. Come out with it—or shall I take it?"

"N-No, your worship, s-surely your worship d-does not m-mean us harm . . ." He reached into the pocket of his voluminous trousers and produced a handful of coins which, with a sorrowful look, he reluctantly gave to the bandit.

He received a menacing look. "Is that all, my friend?"

Mr. Herriot bobbed his head several times, saying between chattering teeth, "Oh, yes, yes, yes, on the soul of my mother, I swear that it is all. It is what we saved f-for many months . . . so my w-wife could visit her old mother who is dying and has s-sent word that . . . that she l-longs to look on her again. These are all our s-savings, your worship."

"Ummmm, it's passing little," the bandit growled. "Turn out your pockets, dog."

"I s-swear to your w-worship . . ." Taking his arm from around Athena and visibly trembling, he obeyed. "You s-see, your w-worship, quite, quite empty. If you t-take this we shall h-have nothing. C-could you not l-leave us a pura or two for ourselves?"

With a look of contempt, Andrutzos flipped two coins at him. "Here, carrion," he sneered.

Mr. Herriot caught the coins deftly and stuttered, "Oh, t-thank you, your worship, thank you . . ."

Andrutzos turned his fierce gaze on Athena.

"What about your woman . . . what treasures does she have concealed about her?"

Athena turned pale. She had never been so frightened in her life. Mr. Herriot's injunction not to speak had been easy to follow. She had a feeling that her voice was stifled in her throat. Mr. Herriot, who had put his arm around her again, said in a quavering croak, "She . . . she has n-nothing. She, too, worked for what I g-gave you, earning it by . . . washing many b-bundles of clothing for t-travelers at the inn. Night and day, she has worked, your worship, night and day."

Behind him, one of the men laughed and said something which, being in dialect, she did not understand, but she was aware that Mr. Herriot had stiffened and that a muscle in his jaw was twitching. Then, Andrutzos moved closer to her, staring down at her. She had not realized how very tall he was, a veritable giant of a man. There was something terrible in the fixity of his gaze; she had seen the stable cat look upon a mouse in that same way, just before it impaled the creature upon its claws. Even as this unwelcome comparison arose in her mind, Andrutzos's hand shot out and fastened on her shoulder, his sharp nails digging into her flesh.

"Ah, no, l-leave my wife alone," Mr Herriot howled.

The bandit tightened his grip—his eyes, a yellow-green like those of a cat, remained on her face. Reaching up, he yanked off her turban and ran a hand through her loosened hair. She shrank from his touch. She was consumed by fear, and she was cold, very cold, so cold—icy cold and, at the same time bathed in perspiration. Her captor nodded, saying softly, "You are right, Kostas. She is young and well-looking, more than that, beautiful, far too great

96

a prize for this miserable dog to have. She needs a man, a real man, one who is strong and brave . . ."

Athena wanted to cry out, but terror had, indeed, robbed her of her voice.

"Oh, p-please, your worship," Mr. Herriot sobbed. "My wife is . . . is . . ." He moved forward, timidly but determinedly tugging at Andrutzos's sleeve.

"Down, dog." With a savage thrust of his elbow to Mr. Herriot's chest, he sent him reeling to the ground. Athena found her voice and shrieked and shrieked again as Andrutzos clasped her in his arms. His odious smell was in her nostrils, his sweaty hands heavy on her back. As she looked into his eyes, her incipient scream emerged as a mere whimper. She tried to turn her face away but, to her horror, his mouth fastened on her lips. Furious she beat against his chest but to no avail—he continued to kiss her, the while his hands slipped beneath her blouse and caressed her. At last, he raised his head. His eyes were gleaming and he was breathing hard, hard as if he had been running a race. He seized her shoulders and pushed her back. She tried to fight against him but was no match for his strength. She fell; as she did, she saw Mr. Herriot launch himself at Andrutzos only to be caught and roughly held by one of the other men.

Andrutzos was laughing again—his horrid laughter once more echoing back at them from the distances. With one huge hand, he pinioned her to the earth—with the other he was fumbling purposefully at his belt while she, filled with a terror greater even than that she had experienced in the last few moments, greater than any she had ever known before, writhed in a futile effort to free herself.

Then suddenly, there was a volley of shots.

With a curse, Andrutzos looked up. Athena heard men shouting—not in Greek. The tongue was Turkish. The soldiers must have caught up with them!

Andrutzos's hold on her loosened; he started to rise but gasped and with a great groan, fell forward. In that instant, Athena saw a grim-faced Mr. Herriot jerk a reddened dagger from the bandit's back and slip it quickly into his sleeve. He pulled her from the man's inert body, then knelt a few paces distant and caught her in a frenzied embrace, holding her against him, kissing her on the cheeks and forehead. Between caresses, he murmured anguished endearments in Greek. His lips were against her ear and he hissed, "Do not struggle. Put your arms around me and weep."

She needed little encouragement for this. The tears were already in her eyes. Huddled in his lap, she gave full rein to them, while he continued to stroke her hair, soothing her and dropping gentle little kisses on her face.

Soldiers crowded about them and one of them knelt down and turned the bandit's body over, another exclaimed excitedly, "Andrutzos!"

"Andrutzos . . . Andrutzos . . ." The name was repeated in awed whispers as the soldiers stared unbelievingly at the fallen man. Grinning and gesticulating, they all began to talk at once. After a few moments, a man who looked to be in command of the troop tapped Mr. Herriot on the shoulder and said something in Turkish.

Mr. Herriot answered brokenly, his voice still filled with terror. He spoke in Turkish, but intermingled with it were Greek phrases. He talked for a long time, while the man listened silently. As Mr. Herriot reached the end of his explanation, he pressed his hand against Athena's stomach and broke into tears.

Daring to steal a look at the officer, she saw him nod and stare at Mr. Herriot contemptuously. Then he barked an order and, to her amazement, the Turks seized the body of the bandit and dragged it away. She glanced across the clearing and discovered that Andrutzos's men had been rounded up. One of them had been shot in the shoulder, another was limping, while the remaining two had their hands tied behind their backs. Prodded by their captors, they were marched out of the clearing while Mr. Herriot continued to clutch Athena, running his lips over her hair and alternately sobbing and continuing his babble of endearments. It was only when they had been gone for some little time that he relaxed his hold on her, saying, though with something less than his usual sangfroid, "I do not believe that they will be back."

Moving a short distance away, she stared down at her hands. "W-what did you t-tell them?" she asked in an unsteady whisper.

"They believe we are two poor peasants who were set upon by the bandits. It is what I hoped would happen, else I should not have appeared so craven. I hoped by my protests to stall for time and I was successful—also I was able to convince the Turks that you were expecting my first-born child. It was not difficult to convince them—for they have made a greater haul than us. Kyriakos Andrutzos is notorious; he and his followers have been terrorizing this part of the country for years. The soldiers will be able to claim credit for killing him—they can expect rich rewards."

The memory of Andrutzos's hands on her body

was in her mind. His odor seemed yet to be in her nostrils and her mouth felt ravaged by his kisses. She had an impulse to cry "Unclean, unclean," as lepers had been wont to do in ages past, and she could not bring herself to look at Mr. Herriot, who had been witness to her shame. She could, however, say in a small voice, "You were very clever. You sounded most convincing. Anyone would have... have thought you were afraid."

"Being afraid helped," he returned grimly.

"You... were afraid?" she demanded incredulously.

"Grievously." He expelled a quavering breath. "I was afraid that the Turks would not get here in time and that... but no matter, they have gone and we are safe, Miss Penrose, at least from those men. They'll not trouble us again—which means that we will have a respite from always having to be on our guard." He paused. "But you are still weeping. I know it was a terrible experience, but it's over."

"It's *not* over," she wailed. "It... it can never be over. He kissed me. He touched me. He... I am ashamed, I am so ashamed!"

"Miss... Athena," he said quickly. Moving closer to her, he commanded, "Athena, look at me."

Her dark locks, loosened from their plaits in the struggle with Andrutzos, were hanging over her face. She was glad of that concealing curtain. "I cannot..." she wept, burying her face in her hands.

Gently he brushed her hair back from her face and put his arms around her. She tried to move away from him, but he held her firmly, saying, "There's no reason why you should be ashamed, my dear. It is only your pride that is hurt, and pride cannot enter into this. You did nothing to invite his embrace. You must try and forget it as I shall have

100

to forget cringing and whining before that rascal, when I longed to drive my knife into his heart!" Fury threaded his tones. Then, in a low, shamed voice, he continued, "I must also forget that I stabbed him in the back—which was the act of a craven, too, but it was the role I was playing and I had no choice. I could not have let him live . . . but all the same, it was a coward's thrust!"

She looked up at him, "Do not dare to call yourself a coward!" she cried. "You were like Ulysses and the Cyclops. The giant was too big, too powerful to kill by any ordinary means and so Ulysses used his wits just as you used yours. You were altogether wonderful, Sa—Mr. Herriot."

He regarded her for a long moment. Then he smiled. It was not like his usual smile. There was no trace of bitterness in his expression, no ironic gleam in his gray eyes. He said, "I do not count myself in quite the same august company as Ulysses, but I thank you for the comparison. However, I must tell you that it was time rather than my wit that saved us." His eyes darkened. "If those soldiers had not been so near, we would have been in a . . . most unfortunate position."

"I do not believe it for a moment," she said decidedly. "I am sure you would have thought of something else."

A gleam of amusement shone in his eyes. "My dear Athena, you will turn my head." He moved away from her. "Now, are you beginning to calm down?"

"Yes, I do feel better," she said gratefully.

"And do you think I was right in what I told you?"

Her cheeks burned, "I . . . yes, Mr. Herriot."

"No," he demurred. "I cannot be Mr. Herriot,

not until we reach our destination. We have roles to play. We are Greeks and also we are husband and wife. Consequently, you must be Athena, a name most apt for this part of the world. However, I cannot say the same for Sable. We must think of something else.

"Ulysses," she said with a watery smile.

"No, it ought to be something shorter . . . Basil, perhaps? That is a name which is much honored here in Greece—it having belonged to one of their Church fathers. Could you accustom yourself to calling me Basil, do you think?"

"Basil . . ." she repeated. "Yes, I could call you that, but—" her voice softened—""I shall continue to think of you as Ulysses."

Seven

"Basil," Athena said experimentally.

As she had anticipated, the bearer of that new name gave no sign that he had heard it. Head down, he was walking a few paces in front of her, picking his way over the rocky ground and moving ever upwards. He had doffed his jacket because of the heat and his damp shirt clung to his back. She wondered if his lack of response was occasioned by his unfamiliarity with the name or because he was trying to deal with the problems that had arisen because of their unfortunate, yet fortunate, encounter with the bandits. She guessed it was the latter reason. He was worried. They had lost much—their money, food and extra clothing. All that remained were the jars of ointment, the bandages and the thin blanket which, for some reason, had been left behind. Thus they dared not continue on the route he had planned. They would need to shelter in one of the small villages that clung, limpet-like, to the sides of mountains. He knew of one such settlement. It consisted of only a few houses and was inhabited mainly by shepherds who eked out a hard living from a few olive trees and from their flocks. These, he had told her with a bitter twist to his mouth, consisted of very few sheep indeed, the Turks having appropriated most of the livestock in yearly raids throughout the country. Consequently, he could not be sure how two indigent travelers would be received, though the people did have an ancient tradition of hospitality to strangers. He could only hope that this, coupled with the tale of their sufferings at the hands of Kyriakos Andrutzos, would gain their sympathy. "Yet, if they do take us in the fare will be very simple and we cannot expect much in the way of accommodations," he had explained ruefully.

"Nothing could have been simpler than that cave," she had replied, "and I do not find myself the worse for having slept there."

He had shot her a wary look. "They are very poor."

"I shan't mind," she had assured him. However, from his attitude, she guessed that despite the fact that they were no longer antagonistic toward each other, he still feared that she might change back into the spoiled and temperamental Miss Penrose of the *Scorpion*. That annoyed her. She had other annoyances. After they had gathered such belongings as remained to them, they had found the stream in the woods and rested beside it. The sight of it, gushing over the smooth, gray, water-carved stones had pleased her. She had been able to wash her face and, more importantly, her mouth, cleansing it of the taint of the horrid kisses which had left her feeling soiled and damaged inside and out. Thanks to the water, thanks to Mr. Herriot's persuasive arguments, she no longer agonized over the incident. Of a truth, he had been wonderfully wise and so kind to her—but, and here was why she was annoyed, he would not let her return his kindness by tending his wound, which, she feared, required rebandaging. He had been roughly treated by Andrutzos. She retained a vivid and painful image of the bandit's elbow striking him in the chest, but he had insisted that he had sustained nothing worse than a momentary loss of breath. She did not believe him. She was beginning to have more than a little insight concerning the workings of his mind.

He was almost fanatically reluctant to be beholden to anyone. That had been evident when he had come out of his swoon in the cave and learned that she had cared for him. To a man of his nature, that faint had been a regrettable sign of a weakness he abhorred. In a sense, his bravery was admirable; but on the other hand she found his penchant for ignoring the demands of his body distressing. He seemed to believe that he was made of iron. No, not iron—steel, the steel of a finely honed rapier or, if she were to think of animal comparisons, he would be a greyhound or an Arabian stallion—beautiful, brave and impatient of all restrictions, one born for leaping ahead rather than pursuing any ordinary pace, one who was proud as well as purposeful. One ... She paused, biting down a laugh. Incredible that she should be concentrating so completely on a man, whom only two days earlier she had actively hated and whom she now admired and ... Surprise widened her eyes and brought warmth to her cheeks. There was another feeling growing within her, one which she dared not name.

"No," she whispered. "It ... it could not have happened so quickly."

It could not be true. It was *not* true. She had forsworn the very thought of that treacherous emotion. It was particularly mad to think of it in connection with Mr. Herriot because, kind and considerate as he had been, there was a distance between them that he continued to maintain. Certainly he had no such feeling toward her. Yet, though she tried to expunge it from her heart, the emotion remained and with it the memory of the "play-acting" for which he had apologized so profusely—his lips on her hair, his kisses on her face, his arms encircling her. At the time she had been too distraught to appreciate it, but she cherished the memory and wished he had not found it necessary to apologize. She wondered what he might have said if, instead of shyly assuring him that she understood, she had told him that she wished it might happen again. Tears rose to her eyes. She did not need to wonder about his reaction. His gray eyes would turn frosty, his lips would compress—he would be the disapproving Mr. Herriot of the *Scorpion* and the *Apollo*.

Last night he had spoken a truth in jest. He had said he must think of her as his employer. She was sure that much of what he had done for her came out of his strong sense of duty. She was woefully certain that he had no feelings for her beyond that. Why should he? He had seen her at her very worst. Probably, he imagined that all her life she had been hurling trays at servants and being generally disagreeable. Furthermore, he must have known about the defection of Eames and, witnessing her actions on board ship, must have believed that the Marquis had had a narrow escape. If only she could find a way to correct those earlier impressions ... but there was little chance of that. They would probably remain with him for the rest of his life. Yet, he had shown *some* signs of liking her ... No, he might have felt sorry for her; and naturally, since they were compelled to travel together, he must feel it incumbent upon himself to be agreeable. After all, they shared a common danger; but once it was over... if it ever *were* over. She frowned. She had not given any thought to their continuing peril. The ruse by which they had evaded their pursuers had given her a false confidence. She had best remember that they were not safe yet. They would not be safe until they came in sight of Athens. There was, he had told her, a monastery on the outskirts of the city where he had stayed many times. Once they were there, no one would trouble them, but between them and Athens were many miles of mountains and plains; he had mentioned such cities as Argos and Corinth.

Forgetting the peril of the moment, she let her thoughts drift to ancient Argos—Jason setting sail with the Argonauts to find the Golden Fleece and receiving the help and hand of the sorceress Medea. Later they had dwelt in the Kingdom of Corinth and Jason had fallen in love with the gentle Glauce, upon whom Medea had exacted so fiery a revenge—poor Glauce, her flesh burning from contact with Medea's poisoned robe, drowning herself in the fountain. How often Athena had read the tale and longed to visit Corinth! Well, she would see it and Argos as well, fleeing like Glauce, from the wrath of an implacable enemy. It was really ironic and she had no reason to feel secure—she glanced ahead and saw Mr. Herriot, whom she must call Basil, and knew herself to feel protected if not loved. How foolish she was to want both when she did not deserve either! If there were only some way of proving herself... She had made up her mind not to complain—and save for her distress over Andrutzos's attentions, she had not—but there was more she wanted to do, help him, really help him, show him that she was not as spoiled and willful as he must believe but . . .

"Athena . . . Athena!"

She glanced up hastily. There had been an edge of impatience to his tone. "Yes . . . Basil?"

Half-seriously, half-jestingly, he said, "I should offer you one of our two remaining puras for your thoughts, though they are not worth so much as a penny."

She looked down quickly. "My thoughts are worth nothing at all."

"They were enough to deprive you of hearing." His smile softened his words. "Now is not a time for contemplation. Our way is rough and you must watch your step. But that is not what I wanted to tell you. Look." He pointed.

Moving to his side, she clutched his arm excitedly. They were on a high rise of ground and, some little distance away, she saw a number of whitewashed cottages clustered together on a hilltop. "Oh, is that the village you've been seeking?"

"Yes . . . and I must warn you. We are Basil and Athena Kristopoulos from Patras and we must be very certain to speak in Greek at all times, even when we are alone. I cannot think that Enver's creatures would have pursued us to this remote eyrie, but we must take care. Also—" a slight redness spread across his cheekbones—"the Greek woman is subservient to her husband and he . . . often gives her orders. If I should seem arbitrary, remember that it is all a part of our disguise."

"I understand," she said in Greek. Falling to her knees, she lifted supplicating arms. "Do not beat me, Master of all Masters. I promise that I shall be good and obey your slightest wish."

He laughed. "I'll not beat you, if you are obedient and . . ." He helped her to her feet. "Let me compliment you on your accent. You have learned the language well."

"I had an excellent teacher," she said softly. "My father."

"On the contrary," he returned, "your father had an excellent pupil."

She fluttered her long lashes at him. "Oh, sir, are all Greek husbands inclined to be so gallant?"

"That," he replied, "should, I believe, depend on their wives." He turned away abruptly. "But come—we are wasting time."

It was a longer walk than she had expected. As they neared the village, she saw slanting cobble-stoned streets stretching up the incline. In a small field, donkeys grazed and on a higher slope she saw the plantings of olive trees. Still higher, a number of goats wandered about. Chickens were everywhere, running up and down between the houses and on the streets. However, she did not see any people: she supposed the women were inside their cottages working and the men were tending their flocks. Then as they came closer Athena saw that the walls of several cottages were caved in and the road strewn with rubble.

"Earthquake," Mr. Herriot muttered.

"Oh," she exclaimed and then came to a startled halt—for an old man had appeared before them, almost as though he had materialized on the spot. He was clad in dark clothes, similar to those worn by Mr. Herriot, but they seemed far too big for a body that looked almost skeletal in its thinness. The head that topped it was similarly skull-like—the skin tanned to the color of old leather was stretched across high cheekbones and fell into deep wrinkled hollows around eyes, which were, however, as sharp and as seemingly fierce as those of Andrutzos. Meeting his gaze, Athena instinctively drew closer to the man she must now call husband.

Mr. Herriot must have guessed her thoughts for he took her hand in his warm grasp and looking up at the old man, said courteously, "I give you greetings, sir."

"And to you greetings, stranger," was the reply. "I am Andreas Suliotis—what might you and your woman be called?"

"Basil and Athena Kristopoulos. We come from Patras."

"A great city." Suliotis studied Mr. Herriot's face. "But what do you do so far from your home?"

Glibly, Mr. Herriot recounted the story he had given the bandit, embellishing it with the treatment he had received at the hands of that same bandit and describing the latter's death, dealt, he was careful to say, by one of the Turkish soldiers.

Suliotis received the news gravely. "It is well that he is dead, my brother—at any other time it would have been a cause for general rejoicing for we, too, have suffered his raids. However, as you see, we have had other misfortunes. Four days ago, the earth shifted its body and great devastation followed. Two of our strongest men are dead and many more are hurt; meanwhile our flocks are scattered and there are wolves loose in the mountains that are preying on them—and too few to corral the sheep and hunt the marauders. Here, alas, are many old men such as myself and children too young to be of assistance. We would be glad of a helping hand, my brother."

"And I shall be glad to offer it," Mr. Herriot

said with a readiness that distressed Athena—he was too tired, she thought resentfully. "However," he continued, "we cannot remain with you long, since we are on my way to my wife's parents, who are old and eager to see their daughter. My wife is expecting our first-born child which is why we came here. We are bereft of food and the money to pay for shelter. We had hoped . . ."

"There is food and there is a cottage which stands empty. Those who lived in it ran forth at the first rumbling and were felled by stones. Ironically, the cottage remained almost intact; you may stay there and we will see that you have some recompense for your labors."

"I would like to help, too," Athena said quickly. "I have some knowledge of nursing." Glancing up, she saw a protest about to form on Mr. Herriot's lips but before he could voice it, she said earnestly, "I want to do it, my husband. Fear not, my time is not for many months."

She was wickedly amused to see him blush. Almost curtly, he nodded, saying, "As you choose—only you must not exert yourself too much." To Suliotis, who was looking at him quizzically, being obviously unused to such husbandly consideration, he said, "She is not strong." Holding up her hand, he continued, "You see that she has been advised not to work and has been much abed in the last weeks."

The old man regarded Athena's white hands and well-kept nails with some surprise, "It . . . it is almost like that of a fine lady."

"My first wife died in childbed," Mr. Herriot explained. "I should not want my little one to do the same." He gave Athena an affectionate squeeze.

"Nor shall I," she said. "My man is over-cautious. I am strong." She did not trust herself to say much more—it would not do for her to burst into the slightly self-conscious laughter that was welling up within her. She was extremely glad when Suliotis, giving her an approving look, said, "I shall take you to my wife—she will give you some tasks to perform. Come, I shall show you where you may stay."

"My man," a woman said proudly, "held the roof from falling on us while we ran out for shelter. He has already repaired it and now is in the mountains looking for the sheep and hoping to shoot the wolves. He is very strong." She held up a dripping shirt and slapped it down in the stream, rubbing it against the stones.

Athena, kneeling beside her, smiled and followed her example. She had not been recruited to tend the sick. She had been told that there were elderly women aplenty to perform such services. Instead, the ancient wife of Suliotis had set her to scrubbing the linens from the bedstead in the cottage she would use. She had also been given clothing both for herself and for Mr. Herriot. That it had belonged to the late occupants of that same cottage had given her a very queasy feeling. She had been on the point of politely refusing the largesse when, fortunately she had remember that at this juncture she was not the rich Miss Athena Penrose but instead the young wife of a poor Greek from Patras, one who had lost all his savings to Andrutzos. Athena Kristopoulos had forthwith shyly and thankfully accepted the offering. Now, as she rubbed them with the strong soap that had also been given her, she was grateful for this unexpected addition to their scanty wardrobes. Her own clothes were dusty and soaked with perspiration and, without doubt, those of Mr. Herriot would be filthy once he returned. Tomorrow, she would come again to the stream and wash them. Silent laughter shook her—she had arrived at that conclusion as easily as if she were accustomed to such tasks! Another flurry of giggles threatened as she tried to imagine her Aunt Caroline's reaction had she been able to see her niece. She would not have enjoyed the sight for long, the vinaigrette would have been brought—indeed Aunt might even have suffered an attack of apoplexy. Jane's reaction would not have been vastly different. At that point, Athena lost all desire to laugh—poor Jane. To think of her was to feel deeply ashamed. Her maid had always washed her garments, washed and ironed them. Each day that she had been ill, the girl had brought her fresh night dresses and . . . But it was better not to remember that miserable time on shipboard, because Ares would enter her mind as well. Poor Ares, what had happened to him? Not knowing was an agony . . . she did not dare dwell on it. Better to follow the example of the women about her.

She stole a surreptitious look at them—there were some ten or eleven of them lined up along the banks of the plashing mountain stream. Most of them were in their late teens or early twenties—but there was a maturity about them that she knew she lacked. They were born to hardship and they aged early. From listening to their conversation, she knew that several had had menfolk injured in the quake, while two had sick children and still others were breeding. Yet, for all their problems, they laughed and chattered among themselves, resolutely or, perhaps habitually, living in the present. She was glad that beyond smiling encouragingly at her they had had little to say to her. Though they were glad to help her, she was yet a stranger, who knew nothing about the gossip of the tiny community; and gossip they did, muttering secrets to each other and occasionally bursting into rich, earthy laughter. To listen to them was to gain new insights.

Athena had always heard that the Greeks were sadly oppressed; she had imagined, too, that they must all be miserable, but these women seemed far from unhappy. Not even the earthquake had quenched their spirits. Thinking of that, thinking of the continuous toil they had known all of their lives, she felt again ashamed. She, Athena Penrose, was there under false pretenses. She had accepted the bounty of Madame Suliotis when she commanded funds that would have kept everyone in that village wealthy for a generation! She wanted to kneel and beg their pardon—then common sense came to her rescue. She might be the wealthy Miss Penrose but, at that moment her riches were out of reach. Indeed, she was even more poverty-stricken than those who worked at her side.

"Aieee, Athena." Her neighbor on her left gave her a jab in the ribs. "You are perhaps dreaming. If I'd not captured it, your wash would have drifted down the mountain." The woman laughed. "But I understand. When I was expecting my first, I too, would find myself falling into forgetfulness. You wait until you have eight little ones to hang on your skirts. You'll be done with dreaming, then."

Athena Penrose felt a blush mount her cheeks, but Athena Kristopoulos shared her neighbor's laughter; and, retrieving her garments, she thanked her and was careful to scrub more vigorously than ever.

It was very late. The sun had descended behind the mountains hours since and Athena, standing in the doorway of the cottage, looked anxiously up a street whitened by a full moon, wondering what had happened to Mr. Herriot. There was chicken and beans, as well as wine and cheese given her by old Madame Suliotis. She had saved the greater part of the repast for him—he would be hungry when he returned—but surely he should have been back before this? Her heart was pounding, her throat aching with fear. He had been very tired when he had gone up the mountain with the other men and being so weary, it would have been all too easy for him to make a misstep and fall down a ravine. If that happened . . .

"You are borrowing trouble, Athena," she said, aping the severe tones of Mrs. Burdgett, her old nurse. She was being silly and childish. He was a man who was well able to take care of himself. Resolutely, she went back to the wide old bed and sank down on it; when she had put the fresh linens on it, she had thought it monstrously hard—now, it felt amazingly soft, but she had no intention of testing it further. She would wait for him and insist that he use it—he with his injuries must have it. Her eyelids were very heavy; it had been a long day. Her bones ached; in addition to the washing, she had swept the cottage and mended some tears in the garments. She wished that she had in the past been more interested in the womanly arts. Her stitches were big and left much to be desired. She *was* tired. If she put her head down just for a second . . .

Andrutzos was clutching her, holding her tight against his hard chest—his sharp talon-like nails were biting into her shoulder and his mouth was fastened on hers—his dead mouth, for he was dead,

dead, dead and cold, his flesh was icy to the touch. She could not escape him. She screamed and on that scream she awakened. She blinked—the room was filled with the gray light of early dawn and she was still lying on the bed. With a feeling of guilt, she realized that she had fallen deeply asleep and he, coming in, had not disturbed her. That meant that he must have slept on the floor; she looked down, but he was not there. He had not come back. Her worst fears had been realized—something had happened to him!

Jumping up she ran to the door, pulled it open and dashed outside. Just as she reached the street, she heard footsteps and turning, saw him coming slowly down the hill toward her. She ran to him, a spate of questions dying on her tongue as she saw his face. His eyes were hollowed, his eyelids drooped; he looked, in fact, as if he were walking in his sleep. Seizing his hand, she said softly, "Come, my dear."

Once in the cottage, Athena pushed Mr. Herriot down on the bed. As he lay back, he gave her a vaguely startled look. "Thena," he muttered, "why you not 'sleep . . . s'late, mus' be starting soon." More than the slurring of his words, the fact that they were in English told her of his fatigue. For Mr. Herriot to forget the precaution he had strictly enjoined upon her, he must indeed have passed the limits of his endurance.

She dared to smooth the tangled hair back from his forehead. It was wet to the touch. "We will start whenever you choose, but first you must sleep."

"No time . . . sleep . . . mus' . . ." he murmured as his eyes closed. He did not even stir as she removed his shoes and pulled the covers over him.

The sun was streaming through the window when Mr. Sable Herriot awakened. Opening his eyes, he looked dazedly up at a battered, white-washed ceiling. It was badly cracked in places and centered by a dark stain which had the aspect of a camel. There was the hump, and there the long neck topped by a small, narrow head. He smiled drowsily. As a child, he had been wont to see shapes in spots on the table linen, in spills on the carriageway and in the clouds overhead—particularly in the clouds. His mother had said fondly ... He frowned; that was all such a long time ago ... He stretched. He felt extremely well-rested, which was surprising; for, judging by the position of the sun, he had been sleeping only about four hours. When he had come down from the mountain, he had been so weary he could not even remember returning to the cottage; yet, now he was totally refreshed! Of course, he had always been resilient. If he had not been able to withstand privation, he could never have endured all that he had suffered since leaving his father's house. His face darkened. He rarely let himself think of the past; yet, in a few moments, he had conjured up two most unwelcome memories. That puzzled him. He was not accustomed to awaken with anything on his mind save the plans of the day and those of this day called for a speedy departure. He had expected to remain longer in the village, but that was not necessary. Not only had he helped the shepherds round up the missing sheep, he had also shot a wolf—right between the eyes and that with an antiquated musket such as he had never handled before. The kill had earned him the admiration of the shepherds and, more important than that, their promise to provide him with food and a little money. He thought of them with gratitude and compassion. They were a little like their own lost sheep, frightened and dazed by the devastation that had happened within minutes. He had left them sleeping on the mountain. He would have remained with them, but he had not wanted Athena to remain alone any longer than was necessary.

Poor, poor child. He shook his head. She had had a terrible experience, but Andrutzos had paid for it. It had been extremely pleasurable to kill him. He grimaced. That was the most painful memory of all, seeing her struggling in the embrace of that villain, while he was unable to go to her aid. Inadvertently, he touched the spot in his chest where Andrutzos had hit him—it had ached off and on most of the day and part of the night, but now . . .

He frowned, realizing that his chest was bare. Athena must have removed his shirt while he slept. He touched the bandage and knew that it had been changed. He exhaled a hissing breath. It was not seemly that she should perform such intimate services, not when he was doing his utmost to be entirely impersonal in all his dealings with her. She seemed not to understand their position. The situation was compromising in the extreme. If any of her relatives or friends were to discover that she had traversed much of Greece, unchaperoned and in his company, her reputation would be lost and he compelled to offer for her. She would not want that and neither would he. It was a damnable position for them both! Her fool of a brother should never have encouraged in her the wild notion of coming to Greece—but there had been no convincing that foolhardy youth of the dangers that lay ahead of them, dangers that even he himself had not foreseen. And look at the outcome. Much as he disliked Ares, he could feel very sorry for him. He might be dead, and if he were not, he must have been hurt. Though that was due entirely to his own folly, it did not make it any less a tragedy. In common with his sister, he had been impetuous, spoiled and ... No, he was not being fair. In the last two days, his opinion concerning the "rich Miss Penrose," as he had mockingly called her in his own mind, had undergone a decided change.

She had managed to surprise him, and very pleasantly, too. The last forty-eight hours had been fraught with peril and for her, sorrow. In that time, she had lost her beloved brother and become a fugitive, yet she had not complained and, he had to admit she had been very helpful. If her attentions to his person had proved embarrassing, he had profited by them—his wound had not festered. Then, during that long journey over the mountains, she had neither caviled at his haste or displayed any fear of following him on that tortuous trail. Indeed, she had refined very little on the horrors of her encounter with Andrutzos.

His teeth clenched. Every time he thought of those terrible moments, he regretted that he could not have strangled the bandit with his bare hands, choking the life out of him slowly—he had died far too quickly. And to have been obliged to speak softly to the rogue ...

His lips twitched into an unwilling smile. She had called him "Ulysses" and praised him at a time when almost any other female would have succumbed to a violent attack of hysteria. He wondered where she was. It was very quiet in the cottage. He had a vague memory of encountering her on the street or had he merely dreamed that, for why should she be on the street at such an hour?

Probably she was still sleeping...but where? He raised himself up on his elbow and then saw her sitting at a small round table, her head bent over something white in her lap, her hands busy. She was sewing! He was glad she was not asleep—that meant that she would soon be ready to go.

"Athena..." he said.

She looked up immediately, smiling at him delightedly, "Ah, good morning, dear husband," she caroled. "You are awake at last." She put her sewing on the table and came to stand at the end of the bed. A little shyly, she continued, "I hope you are feeling better rested."

"I am feeling amazingly well considering that I cannot have slept more than four hours," he said pointedly, resenting her use of the words "at last," almost as if she had begrudged him that brief slumber.

"Four hours?" Her smile broadened and she laughed. He did not quite understand why she had laughed, but he liked the sound of it—it was deep and slightly husky. She was looking very well; she had had a touch of sun and her skin had taken on a golden hue, but why was she regarding him with that peculiar expression? He could define it only as a sort of amused tenderness. Tenderness? He shied away from that particular term, yet, it was apt. One other woman had looked at him in that way— Eustacia Palomides, but why should Athena look at him with Eustacia's eyes? Though he did not feel tired, he must be more tired than he had realized, because he was having great difficulty in gathering his wits about him this morning. She was still standing at the end of the bed, smiling at him in that lovely way. There was a faint flush of pink in her cheeks—a blush? Well, that was understandable—to all intents and purposes, she, a carefully cherished and well-brought-up maiden of nineteen was in his bedroom or was he in hers? He felt himself flush, too. There was no doubt about it, it was a very confusing and unusual situation. Though he could give her ten years and was a seasoned man of the world, he felt strangely ill-equipped to deal with it.

With a certain diffidence, he said, "I hope you slept well."

"Extremely well," she told him brightly. She added, "Are you hungry? We have bread, cheese, apricots and grapes. There is also goat's milk." She wrinkled her nose. "I am not over-fond of goat's milk. Of course, I had it for the first time yesterday morning and it may be that I shall get used to it."

"Yesterday . . . morning?"

Her laughter echoed through the room once more. "Yes." That tender expression beamed from her blue eyes—so lovely a blue, almost violet in hue. "You might as well know, my dear Basil, you have slept the clock 'round."

"I . . . no, that is impossible!" he exclaimed.

"It is not," she contradicted. "For the last twenty-eight hours, you have been the Shepherd Endymion, kissed by Artemis, the moon goddess, into sleep, though I am glad that it did not happen upon the mountaintop and I am even more pleased that you have awakened. As you know, Endymion slumbered for all eternity."

He had to smile at her nonsense, but her news was indeed startling and not at all welcome. "I have never . . ." he began defensively.

"Been so very exhausted," she finished. "It is a wonder that you did not sleep another day, with all that you have done. Yesterday, at the stream, the women were full of your exploits on the mountain." She looked at him admiringly. "You shot a wolf! They were most impressed by your accuracy—as am I. Only one shot! I have received many compliments on the prowess of my 'husband.' I am considered very fortunate to be wedded to such a man—also I have a feeling that several think me unworthy of the honor. They asked for you, hoping to catch a glimpse of you, but I told them you were sleeping and they quite understood."

He gave her a slight worried frown. "But if I was here"—he touched the bed—"where did you sleep?"

"There." She pointed to the floor. "And before you scold me, let me add that I had a blanket and pillows on which to rest; and, having tried that bed the night before last, I am of the opinion that the floor is the softer—the boards are old and full of dry rot, so they give, which that mattress does not. But enough . . . what may I bring you to eat. Would you like a cup of that milk, my lord?"

"You may bring me nothing," he said sternly. "I am able to fetch it myself."

"No, no, no, that would not be Greek." She whirled back to the table and picked up an earthenware pitcher. "Here, a good wife waits on her husband." Pouring milk into a mug, she brought it back to him. "You told me that yourself," she continued, proffering the mug.

Taking it, he smiled. "I certainly did not mean . . ." He paused, staring at her hands—they were reddened and the nails broken. "What have you been doing?"

"What . . . ?" she began; then, following his glance, she gave him a deprecating smile. "Only a little washing. The soap is strong."

122

"Athena!" he exclaimed in horrified accents. "You should not have ... why did you ... it was not necessary."

"But it was necessary," she insisted. Telling him about Madame Suliotis's gift, she concluded, "We needed clean clothes and furthermore, my dear Ulysses, you will be able to use your wits for purposes more important than making up reasons as to why your 'woman' has 'fine lady hands.' Come, will you tell me that it is not a good disguise?"

He looked down suddenly, swallowing an obstruction in his throat. "No, I will not tell you that." Then, unable to restrain himself, he set down the mug of milk carefully and taking her hands, he pressed one and then the other to his lips, saying hoarsely, "You are ... a most unusual female, Athena Penrose."

Eight

Since a certain disastrous night, shortly after he had passed his seventeeth birthday, Sable Herriot had decided that he hated all women and would henceforth avoid them. A year later, the youth realized that the resolution needed modifying. He hated women, yes; but they served a purpose which, if he were to remain healthy, he could not ignore. Consequently, in the course of his wanderings, which had taken him throughout the British Isles, Europe, the Levant and even through the wilder parts of Russia, there had been many interludes of varying lengths. However, with few exceptions, he was careful to pursue ladies of an age at which wisdom prevailed over passion. Though, of course, he had weathered some stormy passages featuring beautiful eyes bedewed with tears, he had always been reasonably sure that once his back was turned, that form of dew had dried even more quickly than its morning counterpart.

At the age of twenty-four, he had met a female who had helped restore some of his lost faith in her sex. If he did not love Eustacia Palomides, he respected her, and she was his first long affair of the heart. As was his habit, he had chosen a lady of mature years; he had never been attracted to the fair young flowers of society. Girls fresh from the schoolroom bored him to distraction and, despite his numerous experiences, he was still a stranger to the deeper promptings of love. In his younger years, he had been too embittered to believe in that passion. Now, as he neared thirty, he had thought himself too old to suffer it. He had prided himself on his invulnerability to it and laughed at friends enmeshed in its toils. When they had described palpitating hearts and other uncomfortable symptoms, he had suggested that they had fallen prey to indigestion. One such conversation and his friends generally confided their woes to more sympathetic ears. Consequently, he was totally unprepared when all the agonies he had derided descended like a cloud of gnats upon his own person.

At first he was inclined to blame his loss of appetite and his scattered pains upon the rough food he was forced to eat as well as on his injuries; but he had dined on less appetizing viands and his wounds were at the itching rather than the aching stage. Furthermore, these sensations only appeared when he was with Athena—rendering their proximity even more untenable. As a man of honor, he could not lay open his heart, could not write the poems that, much to his confusion, occurred to him at odd hours of the day and night, could not send the flowers that might express his sentiments. Instead, he had to keep his feelings bottled up. It was remarkably frustrating. Others would have envied the position of being in sole attendance upon the lady who had come into possession of his heart, and held it in her two roughened hands. It was those same hands which had been partially responsible for the maiden flight of Eros's shaft. Consequently, as was the case with other victims of the malady, he was by turns happy and moody—but, above all, angry because he must needs act as if that arrow had never found its mark. Worse yet, he feared that he was not as successful at the subterfuge as he would have liked.

Meeting Athena's eyes as they walked down the hill and away from the village, he found them softened and understanding—*too* understanding, *too* loving. He longed to ask her to turn away, but that would have been a ridiculous request and besides he did not want her to turn her face from him—he wanted to look at it, drink in its beauty. More than that, he wanted to kiss her lips, her hair, her eyes, even her feet. He found himself wishing that they would fall in with other travelers, because then he would be required to act the role of her husband— true, a Greek husband was notably indifferent in public; but since he was also supposed to be an expectant father ... He snapped his teeth together. Best not to think of that since it activated another set of emotions. Better to remember that it was all hopeless—better to realize that once they reached Athens, she would be the rich Miss Penrose and he naught but her penniless courier. Of course ... He frowned—he could not think of *that*, not even for her. The past was past and it was not possible to make peace—he had not been believed and even ... He came to a halt, looking about him with a frown. He had thought himself going in a definite direction. There had been landmarks he had been instructed to follow—had he passed them?—he did not know. He had been too deep in thought, thoughts that should never have entered his head.

He said, "Athena, did we pass a shrine?"

She gave him a startled look. "A shrine?"

127

"A *wayside* shrine," he emphasized. "It would look like a box and have a picture of the Virgin in it, or possibly an icon. There would be a cross atop it."

"No, I do not believe we did. I was not paying attention, though."

"It must be ahead of us, then," he said with more assurance than he felt. "It would be near a ravine. Those shrines are set there to remind travelers that some poor unfortunate met his death at that spot. Of course, there is always the chance that a passing Turk might have removed it—they hold Christian symbols in abhorrence."

"And I hold *them* in abhorrence," she said. "Or I did," she added self-consciously. "I—I mean . . ."

"You have changed your opinion regarding the Turks?"

She did not meet his eyes, "No, not really, only . . . Of course, I do dislike them. They have no right here. None."

He wondered what she had really intended to say. He wondered if, in common with himself, she felt a certain elliptical gratitude to Mahmood Enver. If it had not been for his aborted attempt to seize her . . . He pulled himself up sharply. He needed to concentrate upon more pertinent subjects. He hoped the shrine would be ahead of them, rather than at a turn of the road somewhere behind them. He said, "We must continue on our way if we are to reach our destination before nightfall." He looked at her and then hastily looked away. He was glad to be able to add, "You'd best follow me, now. The road before us is not well-marked and I must find footholds. Stay close behind me."

"Do you think the earthquake may have tumbled the shrine?" Athena asked some two hours later.

Mr. Herriot turned a worried face in her direction. "Unless we failed to see it," he remarked wtih something less than his usual confidence.

She glanced at the sky. The sun was descending and long shadows marked the mountains. Shards of clouds were coalescing, forming a purple sea banded with golden waves. It was beautiful and, at the same time, awesome. It blended with the great pointed cypresses above them and the high, water-seamed cliffs. Though they were obtensibly going in the direction of a village, she could not believe that they were near any human habitation. Yet she was not alarmed. She was confident that Mr. Herriot would lead them to a shelter before nightfall. Just to be in his presence was to feel safe, just to hear his voice . . . though, since they had left the village, he had been even more silent than was his custom. Indeed, after that moment when he had amazed and thrilled her by kissing her hands, he had had very little to say. Thinking about that incident as she had off and on all day, she could hardly believe that it had taken place. Yet, it had—and there had been a new note in his voice which, though absent now, still echoed in her memory. And she had noticed a change in his attitude, a gentleness which he had never exhibited before. It seemed to her as if he had split into two Mr. Herriots—one, the sardonic gentleman she had known during the first part of the journey, the other, the oddly vulnerable, ardent young man who had stared at her from the bed that morning and accompanied her from the village. As the day had worn on, *that* Mr. Herriot had retreated, but not entirely; there was still a difference about him, one which she could not quite define, but it was there. He . . . A distant rumble dispersed her thoughts. It sounded like thunder. Glancing upwards, she saw that more clouds had appeared.

"Come." Mr. Herriot seized her hand. "It is going to rain. We must make for the cliffs; there's sure to be a cave. There are caves all through these mountains."

Athena stared at him in alarm. Since she was a child, she had been terrified of thunderstorms. The merest hint of one had been enough to send her scurrying into her bedchamber to huddle under the covers, a pillow over her head to shut out that ominous sound. Here, there were no pillows, no roof; and the cave, if indeed they might find one, was at least half a mile distant.

"Be careful now," he cautioned. "There's no path here."

It had seemed to her that there was no real path anywhere, but as he guided her through the thick, spiky vegetation, she had to agree that this was considerably worse than the way they had been going. Thistles scratched her legs and thorns caught at her skirt—but she was more concerned about him. He had insisted upon bearing the entire burden of the pack—larger, now, with food and their extra clothing. Though an examination of his wound while he slept had showed her that it was healing nicely, she did not think he should put too much strain on it. Another, closer, ominous rumble made her shudder. The sky was much darker. The gold had faded from the clouds leaving them black and swelling with rain. Staring at the cliff face, it seemed to her that she saw several gaps that might prove to be caves. She wished there were some way of reaching them immediately, but instead it was becoming more and more difficult to find a way through the dense undergrowth. She cast a despairing look upwards and in that second a jagged bolt of lightning seared the sky; it was followed by an immense clap of thunder. With a moan, she cowered down, burying her face in her hands.

"Athena." Mr. Herriot plucked at her shoulder. "Come, we must hurry. The storm is imminent."

She gave him a shamed and terrified glance, "I cannot." She shook her head. Then, as an even louder crash reverberated through the air, she began to tremble and sob.

"Come." Lifting her in his arms, he carried her toward the cliff.

"Please," she protested. "I am too heavy, you must not even attempt—"

"Hush," he said. "You weigh very little. In fact, I fear . . ." his words were drowned out by a third, even louder, clap of thunder.

Nearly mindless with terror, Athena pressed her face against his chest; she knew she could not have walked. Her limbs could not have carried her. At the same time, the disparate fragments to which her thoughts were reduced were full of regret. She had forever forfeited his respect. His contempt must have returned in full measure. He . . . She moaned. Great sheets of rain were pouring down upon them. He halted and she would have slipped from his arms, but he did not relax his hold on her. Still clutching her tightly against his chest, he staggered to a tree and put her down close to its trunk.

"There's not much shelter here, but as this is a cloudburst, I am sure it will soon be over."

She nodded miserably. Her panic had subsided and in its place was chagrin. The cliff was not far distant. If he had not been burdened with her, he might have reached it and escaped a drenching. "I am sorry," she said contritely. "It is very childish of me to be so afraid of thunder."

His smile was amused and indulgent. "It is also very common. I fear we were remiss; we should have made burnt offerings to Hephaestus that he forge his bolts on another day and to Zeus that he forbear to hurl them, but—" he shook his head—"I fear that it is Pallas Athena who sends the rainstorms."

She managed to produce an answering smile. "I shall pray that she desist."

"As you are her namesake, please do," he urged.

Unfortunately, Pallas Athena was not to be placated; her wrath, once aroused, whirled around them for the better part of an hour before diminishing into a light but steady downpour. After a quarter of an hour, Mr. Herriot said, "I think we had better chance the cliff. It will soon be dark and we cannot stay out here all the night."

"No," she agreed. "I do hope you are not prone to colds."

"Not in the least," he assured her. "But you . . ."

"Never," she said staunchly. It was not true. She had several colds a winter but none of them had ever been serious. However, she did not think she would suffer similarly here—though she was soaked to the skin—it was still warm and would probably be warmer once the rain had stopped.

There were three caves in the cliff and all were easily accessible. "Which of her palaces would Madame prefer?" Mr. Herriot demanded.

"I must let my master decide," she said.

He smiled. "We could draw lots but, no, I think

the center cave is best. It has the larger opening. It would allow considerable daylight to come in and that might discourage bats."

"B-bats?" she quavered.

"Are you afraid of them?"

She nodded. "You must think me an arrant coward," she said miserably.

"No," he said, looking at her in a way that sent little pulses scampering over her whole body, bringing with them an unexpected warmth. Taking her arm, he continued, "Come, we must brave the possible bats before it is too dark to explore our dwelling."

The cave was larger than it had seemed from below. Striking a flint, Mr. Herriot held the flame to a dry branch, thrusting his makeshift torch toward the roof. "I do not see bats nor do I smell them."

"Oh, how beautiful!" Athena breathed, staring at masses of stalactites, some thick and others almost icicle-thin, gleaming in the flickering flame. The floor of the cave was sown with a few large stalagmites and strewn with branches and leaves.

"I think," Mr. Herriot began, "we ought to make a fire. We can dry our clothes and —" He broke off, startled by a long, melancholy howl that echoed eerily through the cave. Immediately upon that mysterious utterance, a large unwieldy shape hopped past them, disappearing into the gathering darkness.

Athena instinctively drew nearer Mr. Herriot, "What w-was that?" she whispered.

Hurling his burning branch into the rain, he slipped an arm around her waist, holding her against him. "Do not be afraid," he comforted. "I think it may have been a wolf, but it was limping on three legs. It must have been hurt."

"Oh." She clung to him for a second and then stepped back. "Poor creature—it probably hoped to shelter from the rain, too."

"Probably." Kneeling, he began to gather dry sticks together. "Let us hope our fire will discourage other wanderers from sharing our quarters."

"Yes." She looked down self-consciously. "I think, too, that if you are not to catch cold, you must soon remove your wet garments."

"As must you."

Their glances locked and they burst into simultaneous, if nervous, laughter. He was the first to speak. "We have no choice. Yet, let me look at the pack. It may be that our other garments will be dry enough to don. They are folded inside the blanket."

"Let us hope so." She stifled a giggle. "Which god shall we solicit?"

"Hera, guardian of hearth and home," he replied as he opened the pack. "And," he said on a note of relief, "she has heard our solicitations; these are only a little damp."

"All hail, goddess!" Athena's giggle escaped.

"I will make a fire and then I shall go further back into the cave and change. You will remain here in the warmth."

"But you ..." she objected. "You must be warm, too."

"Your master has spoken, wench," he smiled and forthwith strode back into the farther reaches of the cave.

"Let me help you," Mr. Herriot said. Taking Athena in his arms, he gently lifted her over a small stream.

She could easily have jumped it, she thought,

but she had ceased to protest such offers. Just to feel his arms around her even so briefly was a happiness she could not forgo. He released her all too quickly, yet, it did seem as if his hands slid from around her waist more slowly than usual, and had he not held her just a bit more tightly, too? Or was it her imagination? Thinking about the previous evening, she exhaled a breath that was, in part, a sigh.

After he had explored the interior of the cave and found that it did not extend very far back, he had insisted that she sleep in those recesses. "It will be warmer," he had insisted as he had spread their sole blanket over a heap of leaves. He had made his own bed near the mouth of the cave. His strict adherence to the amenities was admirable; rather than regretting it, she should have appreciated it. That she did not suggested that she was sadly wanting in moral fiber and also pride. In spite of that moment when he had kissed her hands, he could not feel the same way about her that she did about him—otherwise . . . She coughed and quickly turned it into a laugh. Though no doubt it had been warmer where she had rested, it had been impossible for her to dry her thick hair completely, and during the night she had felt the cold. She had awakened with a scratchy throat. She had hoped that the heat might bake it out of her, but it had not.

"Athena," Mr. Herriot said sharply, "did I hear you cough?"

"No," she assured him hastily, "I laughed—something that occurred to me. Oh, look, those flowers . . . so many of them!" She pointed down the hill at a mass of yellow blossoms. "Would you know what they are called? They are too big to be buttercups and they are not daisies, either."

He scanned her face. "You are slightly flushed."

"So are you," she pointed out. "It is a warm day, and already we have been walking for several hours."

"Are you tired?"

"Not in the least. Have I not proved that I am used to walking?"

"I think I roused you too early."

"You did not rouse me, I was awake."

"Your eyes were closed."

"I was drowsing and that is different from sleeping. Furthermore, it was well we started early; and, since we found the shrine, we should reach the village soon." She had spoken abruptly because, being so close to him, she wanted to touch him, to . . . Whirling away from him, she ran down the hill and knelt to gather a few flowers.

" 'But they withered all when my father died.' " Seated beside Mr. Herriot on a grassy hillock, Athena tossed down a small bunch of drooping yellow blossoms. "I should not have picked them," she said regretfully. "I had forgotten that wild flowers are lovely only while they are growing. Have you ever seen *Hamlet?*"

He put down the piece of goat cheese he had been holding, "I have more than seen it. I have carried a spear in the army of Fortinbras."

"You never told me you'd been an actor!" she cried.

"Once."

"In London?"

"Out of London."

"You are being willfully mysterious," she accused. "Oh, I do wish I might have seen you."

"You'd not have been impressed."

"But you are a good actor. I am sure Andrutzos

went to his death furious because he'd been slain by a lowly peasant from Patras."

"There were no such exigencies when I was on the boards."

"When I was very little, I longed to be an actress," she confided. "But then an incident happened that made me think it was not safe."

"It was never safe," he smiled; then, "but what was your incident?"

"It happened in Covent Garden. I was but nine and Ares eleven. It was our first Christmas in London and the day after, as a special treat, we were taken to see *Richard III*. And—"

"And someone threw a bottle at the stage and knocked the hat off Mr. Betterton," he finished, his eyes gleaming with laughter.

"Yes, yes, yes!" she cried excitedly. "You'll never tell me you were there, too?"

"I was in the two-shilling gallery, directly behind the man who did the hurling of that bottle, and I was near knocked to the stage by the ensuing riot."

"Oh, I pray you were not hurt!"

"A few bumps." He shrugged.

"Were you acting, then?"

"I was reading law in the Temple."

"Are you a lawyer?"

He shook his head. "No. I found work that was more felicitous."

"Your writing, of course! I do wish I'd read some of your books."

"When we are returned to England, I shall send you some."

"Oh, that . . . that would be lovely," she said in a small voice. She looked down quickly, tracing a little pattern in the dirt. England had been very far

137

from her thoughts. His choice of words indicated something else that had even been farther from those thoughts—separation. He had said "send" instead of "give." On the face of it, a small difference —but it was not small, it was immense, shattering in its implications. Eventually, they would come back to England and his debt to Ares would be canceled —might be canceled already if . . . But she did not want to contemplate that "if," nor did she want to think of England yet. They were still in the middle of Greece—miles away from their destination, which meant that she had days and weeks—possibly months—to spend in his company. She looked around; he was no longer sitting beside her, but standing.

"I hope you are rested. We ought to be on our way."

"Oh, yes, I am quite rested," she assured him, rising immediately. She had the beginnings of a headache and her throat was more than merely scratchy, it was quite sore but fortunately she was not yet hoarse. If she contemplated another long journey with some distress, she was determined that he would never know it. Summoning a bright smile, she ran down the hillock.

She did not know how long they had been walking when she saw the ring of cypress trees. It felt as if they had been on the road forever. Her head was aching badly and she was very glad that he was several paces ahead of her. She was also pleased that since their rest, he had been extremely silent. She feared that if she talked too much, her voice would become as ragged as her throat felt. Because she had been chilled the night before, her cold had developed more rapidly than usual. Her whole head throbbed, and from past experience she knew that it would soon be very difficult for her to breathe. It was getting on toward four or five in the afternoon and at such times, her colds always grew worse—even those which were in the early stages. She fixed her mind on the cypresses. Though she had seen many, she had never found them growing in what appeared to be a perfect circle. Her mother had loved cypress trees. "They always look so trim, even in the wilderness," Lady Penrose told her once. "I shall always think of Greece whenever I see a cypress."

A verse from *Twelfth Night* ran through her head:

> Come away, come away death,
> And in sad cypress let me be laid;
> Fly away, fly away breath;
> I am slain by a fair cruel maid.

She giggled; her own breath was certainly flying away, but she did not like to think of death, and those cypress trees were not sad. As her mother had said, they were trim and she loved that shade of green—dark and mysterious, if one could call a color mysterious. One could certainly call a man mysterious. She thought of Mr. Herriot's brief confidences—he had been an actor and had studied law and had had some success as a writer—but none of these were the sum of the man. What else had he done or been? And why, when he was so brave and strong, bold and handsome too, did she imagine that there was something lost and needful about him? He would hate it if he ever guessed she entertained such a notion. He would regard it as a grievous insult. If ever a man prided himself on his self-reliance . . . ! She laughed. Then she stared—she had seen the gleam of something white between the cypress trees.

Despite her fatigue, she quickened her steps, passing Mr. Herriot and not heeding his startled, "Athena!" as she ran to the grove, and slipping past the trees to find what she hoped might be there—a ruin. Three tall white marble pillars rose from a round base in the center of which stood a broken pedestal. Then, to her amazement, she saw a long crate, half open, lying some three or four feet away. Upon examination, she found that a marble torso sheathed in carefully sculpted draperies lay within it. Near the crate was a beautifully sculptured marble arm and next to it a marble hand, two of its fingers missing.

"Ah." Mr. Herriot strode into the clearing. "The collectors have come and gone, I see."

"The collectors?"

He glanced at the side of the crate. "Exactly. Read this," he pointed.

Wonderingly, she looked down at some roughly penciled letters. "E–L–G–I–N" she read. "Lord Elgin?" she asked confusedly.

"The same. One of his workmen must have left it behind. I have seen a great many similar crates at other sites. And, as you know, a great many of his finds are lying at the bottom of the sea . . . when that vessel he chartered sank."

"Oh." She looked at the broken pedestal. "But he should not have taken it away . . . and to leave it broken. It is a desecration."

"Yes. In the old days, if a temple were despoiled, the gods were angered. Pallas Athena turned one impudent and imprudent nymph into a Gorgon and called her Medusa. These days, similar

140

deeds are rewarded. Lord Elgin and others like him will have an honored niche in history. It has become a business; there are sales of artifacts in Zante and other islands."

"Yes, I have heard that," she said. "Have ... you ever been to them?"

"Several times. I have always hoped I might have enough money to buy back some of them and return them to their proper place, but they have always been beyond my means."

"Oh!" tears filled her eyes, as she remembered Enver's accusations and her own belief in them. Moving away from him, she ran her hand over one of the pillars. With a little sob, she added, "The poor temple!" she was glad he could not read her mind and divine the real reason for her tears.

He followed her. "Do not mourn, Athena," he said gently. "They may plunder her temples and ravish her earth—but that which is Greece is of the mind and heart and spirit and can never be destroyed."

"Oh." She looked at him with shining eyes. "How well you have put it and how right you are." Impulsively she added, "Do you know, Mr. Herriot, I am glad of that riot in Patras. There is so much I should not have known about Greece and ..."

Their glances met. "I, too, have learned something, Miss Penrose," he began, then frowned and shook his head. "But it grows late and—"

"Sable." Athena caught his arm. "Please, let us not leave yet. It is so beautiful here, an enchanted glade and I—I wish to ..." Her voice turned husky and she coughed, a harsh tearing sound that hurt her throat.

"Athena ..." His hand was on her forehead. "You are passing warm, too warm ...."

"Exertion," she assured him. "I do have a tiny cold, but it is nothing."

"It did not sound like nothing. The temple is ... or rather was a famous landmark. The village cannot be more than a league away. Can you walk?"

"Of course I can walk," she said indignantly. "In the words of one Mr. Sable Herriot, an intrepid gentleman of my acquaintance, I do not walk with my head or my eye—or my throat—and my feet are well able to bear me. I could even be Atalanta and run were there a golden apple for a prize and the assurance that I should not eventually be turned into a lion."

His relief was evident as he said, "Then let us be going."

She nodded and kept her head down as they walked from the glade. She did not want him to see the distress which she feared might be mirrored in her eyes, the distress and the anger. It was ridiculous to be angry with a throat, but the throat had produced the cough and before that had happened, there had been something else she had been on the point of confiding. Now those words were gone and her courage with them.

Nine

It was very warm in her room. Through the window, she could see the moon—its whiteness looked cold. She wished she might be able to touch it, because it would, she was sure, prove frosty. A handful of frost against her throbbing head and the pain would go away. "Mama, Mama..." She stretched out her hand. "Water... might I have some water?"

The shape beside her bed rose and moved away. Soon water was held to her lips. She tried to swallow, but it hurt to swallow. There was a large amount of water in her mouth, but it would only trickle down her throat, drop by drop, down her throat, because her throat did not want it. Her throat did not like her. "Mama, Mama..." she moaned fretfully.

"Yes, child," it was only a whisper, but it was very comforting. It pleased her to know that her mother was with her. She had gone away some time ago and Athena had not expected her to return, but she had. "Mama, I have gone to Greece just as you wished." She frowned. Something was wrong, but she did not know what it was—something about her mother and Greece. Oh, yes, her mother loved

Greece and she would be pleased she was there. Yet why was it necessary to tell her mother she was there when her mother was sitting at her bedside? There was something else she wanted to tell her— something very important that she had longed to confide. "Mama, I love . . ." she began and paused. She should not tell her mother that she was in love because it was proper for the man to offer for her first—and afterwards, she could tell her mother that she had loved him all along. One did have to remember the proprieties.

It was really very warm and she wished her head would stop aching. It was not a sharp ache, it was dull. She wished, too, that when she shut her eyes, she would not see such strange visions—ugly men with knives protruding from their backs and shattered statues and Ares. She wondered why Ares should be near the statues in his dreams, appearing and disappearing, so odd of him. "Where are you?" she called hoarsely.

"Shhhh . . . try to sleep," her mother whispered.

"But Ares, Mama . . . I saw Ares and now he has gone. Where did he go?"

"He will be back," came the whisper.

"Will he?" she asked doubtfully.

"Soon."

"Oh, I shall be glad to see him. Oh, I am so warm. It is odd to be warm when it is midwinter. Could you get me some frost from the moon? I love him, you know. I should not tell you that until he has offered for me. I know Papa will not approve my loving him first before anything is said. Though I do not know if . . . if he loves me . . . such a sharp jab on the chest, Mama and he fell back . . . he kissed my ugly hands, so red, so red . . . and the soap burned . . . it made them ugly and he kissed my hands. I think he likes me, Mama . . . but he said he would send them to me, not give them to me and if I do not see him again . . . oh, it is so warm. Why is it so warm when I am so cold? Too much frost on the moon . . . oh, that feels better, Mama. Your hands are gentle . . . *Mama, why am I talking to her—she's dead.*" The knowledge smote her like a hard blow. "Yes, she is dead and I have been talking to her? No . . . oh, that does feel pleasant, thank you." Someone was sponging her face. Her eyelids felt heavy. She had the impression that she had been doing a lot of talking, but of a sudden her head was much clearer and she no longer wanted to talk, she wanted to sleep. She had had difficulty in sleeping, but now she believed she could.

From the experience of five troubled nights, the man by Athena's bed could tell she had finally fallen into one of the semi-stupors that left her exhausted and debilitated. She had had very little real rest in the last week and her fever had shown no sign of reaching its crisis. Rising, he paced back and forth across the room. Though he had had some experience in treating illnesses of this nature and had suffered fevers himself, her condition terrified him. She was so weak; her skin looked almost transparent. As he recalled the reason for her present agony, he slammed a fist into his open palm. It should not have happened. She would have recovered easily enough if it had not been for that ignorant numbskull who dared to call himself a doctor!

"An hour, I was not even gone an hour," he muttered. Incredible that in so short a time, so much that was terrible had taken place! He had brought her into the village and a kindly woman had offered to look after her while he went to the mayor to seek work—he needed to earn the price of a donkey and cart, Athena's cold having convinced him that she was not able to keep up the grueling pace of the last few days. In his absence, the young daughter of the house had noticed she was running a fever. Being an interfering chit—he shook his head, he had no right to be enraged at her—she had been well-meaning and concerned, while that quack she had summoned had been equally well-meaning. Upon examining her, he had immediately set about following the time-honored method of drawing the impurities from the system—he had bled her! God knew how much he had taken. She had looked so white when he had returned and what had come close to breaking his heart was her apologetic glance as she had murmured, "I tried to tell them I did not want to be bled, but they'd not heed me and I . . . I was too tired to protest. I am sorry, Basil."

She had been sorry when it was all his fault! He should have realized that she was too delicately bred to withstand so long and so hard a journey but, yet how could he have foreseen that they would be robbed? If they had been able to hire horses, they might have been well on their way to Athens by now, but it was no help to think of that. His frustration increased. To be so close to aid and be unable to command it . . . ! Under other circumstances, he could have called upon any one of many Turkish officials in these provinces, but he dared not alert them to his presence—Mahmood Enver cast a long shadow. Consequently, he had been forced to retain his disguise and in the character of a poor Greek, he had labored in the fields, helping to bring in the cotton harvest. He had had one stroke of luck; the woman who had first sheltered them had found them an unused hut, even smaller than that which they had occupied at the other village. However, it had a door, a window and a roof. A daughter-in-law of the so-called doctor had furnished a bed for Athena, while he himself slept in the far corner on a straw pallet. He did not mind the hard work or the primitive conditions, but what he did mind was earning so little in the way of money, for some of it went for food and some, a mere pittance, to Elena, the girl who relieved him while he snatched a few hours of sleep. When Athena recovered, she would need—

A tap at the door roused him from his thoughts. Taking a tallow lamp from the table near the bed, he opened the door to Elena, thin, with big kitten-eyes and aged no more than fifteen years but, as she had told him with great pride, married a year and expecting what she firmly designated as her first-born son at the end of the winter. Giving him a shy greeting, she hurried to the bed, putting a gentle hand on Athena's forehead.

"You will find her much the same," he said wearily. It was time for him to go to his pallet, but he was far too restless.

Elena kept her hand pressed on Athena's brow. Then she faced him. "She is not the same," she whispered.

"Not . . ." A ghastly fear seized him. In one step he was at her side. "Not the same?" he repeated. "What do you mean? You cannot be telling me that she—that she's—"

"No, no, no," Elena said hastily. "She is for the first time sleeping well. The crisis has passed. I think now she will begin to recover. It was so with me, last year, when I had such a sickness."

Hardly daring to believe her, he placed a trembling hand on Athena's forehead. As Elena had said, it was cool. The fever had abated. He moved back quickly and strode from the cottage. Then, as he had not done since his mother died, fully sixteen years earlier, he sank on his knees and, burying his face in his hands, began to weep.

Under a cloudless sky and a bright, burning sun, the white-tipped plants wavered in the heat, giving the impression that they were caught in a breeze, but there was no breeze that morning. The men harvesting the cotton blossoms moved along the rows quickly. By midday it would be too hot to work.

Sable Herriot stared across the fields with foreboding. Many of the plants were denuded. Soon there would be an end to his labors and he very little the richer for them. If it had not been for that, he would have been relieved that he was no longer needed. He had come to regret every moment he could not be with Athena. Since his experience that first day, there was always a nagging worry that they would not heed his instructions and leave her in peace. He knew he was being over-anxious. There was nothing more they could do to her. She was getting better.

In the three days that had passed since the crisis, she was looking much more like herself—the hoarseness that had clouded her voice had gone and more important than that, she was breathing normally. Still, she looked very fragile. She needed proper care, the sort of care that only skilled nurses could give her. She needed to be in a comfortable bed in a large, well-appointed chamber, such as she had known all of her life. He thought longingly of Selim Baki, the son of a Pasha, with whom he was reasonably friendly. Yet Enver would stand between them, too. It was two weeks, lacking only a day, since they had fled Patras—were they still being hunted?

He ran his hand over his brow. It was unusually warm this morning, or perhaps it only felt that way because everything seemed suddenly too much for him. He had never been so powerless, so much a victim of the Fates—or was "Furies" a better description? A mirthless smile twisted his lips. There were a number of people who believed that Sable Herriot was far too self-confident. He had never done anything to correct this impression. He had always been confident that he could fend for himself. The knowledge that he had been mistaken was hard, very hard to accept. He was not a man to whom humility came easily; his great sense of pride had never failed him until now, now when he needed it more than ever. Compressing his lips, he knelt down and began to strip the nearest plant of its yield. He had no time for soul-searching but, perhaps, he told himself wryly, that was just as well.

Dogs were barking, men were shouting, women were chattering and children screaming. The fields were never quiet; but surely, Mr. Herriot thought, this uproar was more sustained; and because it was not far distant, he found it particularly irritating. Looking in the direction of the sounds, he saw that two men from the field, several women and children, who had been stuffing the cotton into sacks, were gathered about a man on a great black horse— a fine beast, one that could have borne Athena.... He tensed. It was far too fine an animal to belong to anyone from this poor district. Impossible to see the face of the rider—was he a Turk and if so, why had he ridden into the village? Was he searching for them? He rose and moved forward cautiously and, kneeling behind a row of still-flowering plants, tried to hear what the man was saying. Since everyone was talking at once, the words were barely decipherable. Then, incredulously, he heard a very loud, very irate, "Damn it, is there none here who speaks English?"

Mr. Herriot leapt to his feet and crossed the remaining distance on a run, stopping at the edge of the gathering. The man on horseback was in his thirties and clad in well-cut riding clothes. He looked hot and furious as he continued in even louder tones, "I have lost my interpreter. Cannot any of you understand me?"

Hardly trusting himself to speak, Mr. Herriot stepped forward. "I understand," he said.

The rider's angry eyes fell on him. In them was an expression of relief mingled with distaste. "At last," he growled. "Thank God one of you has a modicum of intelligence."

Mr. Herriot was startled. Evidently the man had taken him for a Greek, but then, he realized, he must not appear much different from his fellow workers who had easily accepted him as one of themselves. He was burned brown by the sun and his two-week beard and moustache, though thin, were bristly, giving him, he supposed, a villainous look which, coupled with his rough, sweat-stain garments and dirty hands, strengthened that impression. It was, he realized tardily, dangerous to identify himself. Since the rape of the temple, the English were not popular in the village. There had been a real problem when Athena, in her delirium, had babbled in English. In case they had recognized the tongue, he had hastened to explain that she was a lady's maid who had lived in England but was of Greek heritage. He moved forward now, saying in heavily accented English, "Yes, I understand a little."

"Thank God," the man muttered. He dismounted. "I am in a most unfortunate position, my good man. My interpreter was taken ill some leagues back. Had to leave him behind. I have two workers, neither of whom understand a word I say to 'em. I find, moreover, that I have been grossly misled. I was told that near this village was a spot where one could make an important archeological discovery, but I find that that damned Scotsman Elgin's been here before me and . . ."

Mr. Herriot gave him a blank look. "You speak slow, please . . . I no understand well." He glanced about him at the interested bystanders. "If . . . will come to trees yonder, where is more cool?"

"Yes, yes, yes, very well," snapped the Englishman. "You lead the way. You understand that?"

Mr. Herriot nodded several times. Turning to the people behind him, he said, "I will give him advice. I know a few words of his tongue."

"Good, good," one of the men said, moving away. To his relief, the others followed. Knowing their curiosity concerning strangers, he had been half afraid that they would trail after him, but fortunately, the harvest occupied first place in their thoughts.

"Well, I must say that you showed uncommon good sense, my man," observed his companion as they came under the shade of some plane trees. "It's damnably hot here . . . damnable country on the whole."

"It's not very like England," Mr. Herriot commented, "but I believe you do the Greeks an injustice in implying that they lack sense. However I know them better than you." He smiled as the man stared at him, his mouth hanging open.

"You're B-British!" he exclaimed.

"Sable Herriot. And you . . .?"

"S-Sable Herriot! The author? But I have read your books on Greece and the L-Levant . . . fine pieces of work. I have used them as my guides . . . . What in God's name are you doing—but hold, I am Geoffrey Farnill, from Oxford." He stretched out a hand. "Oh, I say, this is the most astounding piece of luck and . . . and an honor besides."

Mr. Herriot, clasping hands with his admirer, took a moment to swallow a lump in his throat before he could reply. "I must tell you that it is more than fortunate for me, Mr. Farnill, and also . . . I must change my opinion regarding the activities of the Fates."

"What do you mean? And why were you working out there in that field? And—"

"Come and let us exchange confidences and see if we can be of mutual assistance to each other." For the first time in two weeks, Mr. Herriot was conscious of a surge of happiness unfettered by doubts and dismay.

The donkey cart, drawn by a small gray female, who answered very infrequently to the name of Dryope, jolted along at a slow pace. Athena, lying on the heap of sweet-smelling straw that Mr. Herriot had piled in it before leaving the small inn that stood just beyond the borders of Eleusis, could hear Mr. Farnill's droning voice. She smiled. He was an incessant talker, discoursing prosily upon the state of Greece; on the Turks, whom he respected but could not abide; upon the Greeks, whom he disrespected and could not abide; on Elgin, a pet hatred, because he seemed to have pillaged the country of everything he, Mr. Geoffrey Farnill, fellow of Worcester College, Oxford, would have liked to claim for his seat of learning. Having been founded a scant ninety-six years earlier, it was sadly lacking in the endowments lavished upon those institutions which traced their origins back to the thirteenth, fourteenth, fifteenth and sixteenth centuries.

However, in common with Mr. Herriot, Athena could not find it in her heart to criticize the scholar for an attitude she abhorred. Even if he did believe that the present-day Greeks had nothing in common with the giants of the Golden Age, even if he made the error of thinking that these debased people had no appreciation for their antiquities and did not deserve to possess them, he was still the man who had rescued Mr. Herriot and herself. Mr. Herriot had told her frankly that if it had not been for Farnill's timely appearance in the village, he did not know how they could have survived. Of course she did not believe that. She was serenely sure that he was equal to any disaster, but still, she was grateful to Mr. Farnill. For he, faced with a situation that might have given many a traveler pause, had readily agreed to help them. That this was again due to Mr. Herriot, she had no doubt. Mr. Farnill admired him as an author—but whatever the reason, he had provided them with the means to get to Athens and, in less than half a day, they would be arriving at the monastery of Daphni, where Mr. Herriot, who was acquainted with the Prior, hoped to find someone who could provide accommodations for her.

The sound of hoofbeats was in her ears and Mr. Herriot, mounted on the fleet chestnut mare of Mr.

Farnill's providing, rode up. There was anxiety in his eyes as he said, "I hope this road has not proved too rough for you."

She eyed him with an anxiety that equaled his. He was always so concerned for her, but her main concern was for him. The dark growth of beard that covered his face could not disguise the fact that it had grown much thinner and that new lines had appeared on his forehead. Once, when he had doffed his turban, she had seen streaks of white in his dark hair; she was positive none had been visible before their flight from Patras. She could wish that he had not deemed it necessary to maintain his disguise and act as a Greek interpreter. He needed to rest after all his hard labor. Still she reluctantly had to agree that it was the wisest course, as Mr. Farnill's manner toward him was so overbearing that no one would question their status. Furthermore, the firman that Mr. Farnill had obtained for himself and his other interpreter had sufficed for the two of them, while she was regarded as Mr. Herriot's young sister, who had joined them at his "native" village. They had had a very easy journey, their one moment of tension had come at the border between Argos and Corinth, when several Turkish soldiers had examined their papers with what had seemed to Athena to be suspicious eyes, but it had come to naught. At the other borders, Mr. Farnill's obvious belief that a British passport could get him and his entourage a safe-conduct through Hell had impressed numbers of bored officials, who had let them go without further argument.

"Athena!" Mr. Herriot's voice was sharp with concern. "Did you not hear me?"

She shot him a self-conscious glance. "Oh, yes, of course I did. No, the road is not too rough. I am sorry that I did not answer immediately. I was thinking . . . it is so hard for me to believe that we are actually safe."

"It is also difficult for me," he responded.

"But what will happen when I have reached Athens?" She looked at him anxiously. It was the first time she had put that question to him, mainly because she was a little afraid of what he might answer.

He hesitated. "We shall have to see if your brother has been located and . . ."

"And if he has not . . . ?"

Again, he hesitated. "We shall need to make arrangements," he said more vaguely than usual.

She was on the point of pressing him to explain those arrangements, when Mr. Farnill galloped back. "I say, Basil, there are a great many antiquities to our right. I should not be surprised if we'd not reached the so-called 'Mouth of Hades!'" He spurred his horse forward.

"Oh," Athena cried excitedly, "I should like to see that." She clutched the side of the donkey cart and she pulled herself up, only to experience a swimming sensation which caused her to sink back quickly.

"You're ill again?" Mr. Herriot demanded anxiously.

"No . . . we went over a bump in the road, did you not notice? I lost my balance," she lied. "You know that I am much better."

"And will be better yet, once you've had the time to rest on a proper bed instead of the wooden pallets they furnish for the discomfort of travelers at these wretched Turkish khans!"

"I have not minded them. I found it interesting to stay at those khans. They might not be comfortable, but at least they are safe."

He smiled at her. "Did you not think it ironic to be safe in a Turkish inn?"

"Basil!" yelled Mr. Farnill. "There's a great lot of artifacts lying about on the ground yonder . . . do you think I might have our workers dig down . . . ?"

"Not on the sacred way!" Mr. Herriot called, spurring his horse forward.

Athena looked after him wistfully. She would have preferred him to be more specific about "arrangements." There was only one arrangement she wanted him to suggest and that, of course, entailed an offer. Somewhat to her dismay, he had told Mr. Farnill they were first cousins. Even so, Mr. Farnill had been shocked at the idea of a young man and woman traveling together, without even an abigail to act as chaperone. However, he had subsequently agreed that, given their perilous situation, an abigail would have been an unnecessary encumbrance. He had finally allowed that they had had no other choice than to flee Patras together and he had even told them that, had he been a member of the family, he would quite understand.

She wished that Mr. Herriot had not deemed it necessary to claim that relationship. It was not that she wanted him to offer for her because she was compromised. She thought—she hoped—she was even reasonably positive—that his feelings for her were similar to those she entertained for him. Elena had marveled over the devotion of her "husband."

"Night after night," she had informed a convalescing Athena, "he stayed beside your bed, resting very little, even though he worked so hard in the fields. You are fortunate to possess the love of such a man."

"The love . . ." She had thought herself fortunate, too, the most fortunate woman in the world. Yet, since they had been traveling with Mr. Farnill, she had been aware of a coolness in his manner. With the scholar present, she could understand that —but even when he was not present, there had been a diminishing of the camaraderie they had shared in the last weeks. She had waited in vain for the chance touches, nor had she seen the tender looks that she had glimpsed in his eyes on the morning he had kissed her hands and when he had ecstatically told her that she was out of danger. Could there be a chance that she was wrong? Suppose he had only been doing his duty as a courier? No, that was not possible; she knew he loved her.

She did not think, however, that he could possibly love her as much as she had come to love him. Her mother had once told her that men did not have such deep feelings. "Even though your father is devoted to me, child, I am not his whole life." Of course her mother had been wrong—she had been her father's whole life and he had killed himself in order to join her in death. She did not think Mr. Herriot loved her that much, but she . . . "If anything were to happen to Mr. Herriot . . . to dearest Sable," Athena whispered, "I should only wish to die. Without him, my life would mean nothing."

"Athena." Mr. Herriot had galloped up to the donkey cart again. "Look, we are passing the ruins. If you sit up, you will be able to see the Mouth of Hades. Kneel and I will take your hand. Here you, Nicos!" he yelled to the man who was driving the cart, "stop!" As the man obeyed, Mr. Herriot edged his horse alongside the cart.

She held out her hand and thrilled to his grasp.

"Thank you," she murmured. Then, seeing the jagged and cavernous hole in the rocks, surrounded by shards of broken marble and a whole field of headless torsos and broken columns, she shrank back. Even though she did not believe in the myth, she felt oddly chilled. It seemed to her that the landscape had darkened, but, looking up, she found the sun as bright as ever. She glanced at Mr. Herriot, but he was staring at the cavern. She wondered what he was thinking—she did not want to know. She had an odd presentiment that the chill she had experienced boded no good for her—for either of them.

The monastery of Daphni dated back to the Byzantine era, Mr. Herriot had told Athena. "The name means that it was built on the site of a sanctuary sacred to Apollo. You'll find a laurel grove nearby—in memory of the nymph Daphne, who was, you must recall, changed into a laurel tree to—"

"To avoid the attentions of Apollo," she had said a little indignantly. "Of course, I know the legend well."

"Of course, you would," he had smiled. "What you may not know is that the church of the monastery used to contain some very valuable mosaics. One, in particular, was famous for its workmanship. It was a representation of Christ, but the Turks shot out its eyes."

"Oh, how terrible. Why?"

"Because they feared His gaze. The Islamic religion forbids the painting of portraits. I imagine it is a superstition like that of the Coptic Christians who defaced the heads of gods in the Egyptian temples because they thought the soul of the god was looking down upon them and would curse them for having abandoned the old religion."

"Very interesting and spoken like a true guide," she had teased him gently and they had both laughed, but beneath his laughter had been the chill. There was no denying it, there was definitely a distance between them; and though she tried to dismiss the idea, she feared that he was reverting to the Mr. Herriot whose services her brother had won on the turn of a card.

Her mood was magically dispelled as she saw him come riding up to the cart. "The monastery is just ahead." he said.

She pulled herself up and saw a high wall behind which loomed a tree-crowned hill. "But where is it?"

"Beyond the gates and at the foot of that hill. The walls are there to keep the monks in and the Turks out." He paused, then possessed himself of her hand and held it tightly, saying in a low voice, "*Soon*, Athena."

Before she could respond, he had wheeled his horse away and rode up to join Mr. Farnill.

"Soon . . ." she repeated, while a little thrill of happiness ran through her. It seemed to her that that one word had conveyed a very great deal.

The heavy-set monk who guarded the gates of the monastery peered cautiously through a grill as the bell clanged a second time. Seeing the dark-visaged Greek in garments that were considerably the worse for wear, his small eyes narrowed suspiciously, then widened as he exploded into a huge, rollicking laugh when the unprepossessing traveler remarked in a voice he knew well, "Greetings, Brother Lazaros! I see that your multitudinous worries have worn you to a mere shadow."

"By all the saints," the monk chortled as he opened the gates, "I'd not have known you, Herriot."

"Nor I myself, Brother Lazaros," Mr. Herriot returned as he beckoned Mr. Farnill to follow him into the wide tree-shaded courtyard. "This gentleman, in common with myself, is seeking accommodations. Do you believe that there are any available?"

"Well," the monk began, "we have a preponderance of English visitors here and, of course, it is the Prior's decision, but when he sees that you stand sadly in the need of a bath and some good food, I should think, Mr. Herriot, that—"

"Herriot!"

Both Mr. Herriot and Mr. Farnill were startled by the loud and angry cry that echoed through the courtyard. A tall man, leaning on a cane, limped out of a door a few feet away.

As he made his way toward them, Mr. Herriot stared at him in shocked recognition, biting down an exclamation of pity—for it was Ares who was coming toward them, but how changed! The side of his face was seamed by a livid scar that ran from his hairline to his chin and the once, almost-classic contours of his nose were flattened from a break that had been set badly or not at all. Facing him, Ares glared at him. "You damned coward!" He spat the words out. "What have you done with my sister?"

Ten

The massive pillars of the Parthenon were the color of old yellowed ivory, Athena thought as she leaned against one of them. Mr. Herriot had failed to mention that, but he had told her very little about the antiquities of Athens. She winced and bit her lip. She ought to try to expunge him from her mind. She gazed at the distant Aegean, brightly blue under the October sun. It was a beautiful sight, but like so many other beautiful sights, she took no joy in it. Since that disastrous day at the monastery, three long weeks ago, she had found no pleasure in anything. Her heart was heavy in her breast, which was odd—one would think that a heart that had been shattered into tiny pieces would be lighter. She shrugged the fancy away and continued to stare at the sea. On the morrow, she would be sailing upon it. Depending upon the winds, they should be in England in a matter of two months. "In time," Ares had told her yesterday, "to join Sir Harry at Clifton-Bastle."

She had looked at him perplexedly, trying to understand what he meant. Both names had been completely obliterated from a memory which still centered about Mr. Sable Herriot. Despairingly, she wondered how she could face life without him, but she must. He did not want her. After that meeting with Ares at the monastery, he had vanished from her ken, though she knew him to be still in Athens. Each time she had gone forth on its streets with her brother, she had surreptitiously searched the crowds for a sight of his tall figure. This morning, she had watched the numerous travelers wandering about the ruins of the Acropolis, hoping against hope that she might glimpse him—but again she had been disappointed. She wished she had not let Ares persuade her to come. Even though she understood, even though she had forgiven him for his outburst at Daphni, she could not feel the same toward her brother, nor could she enjoy his company. He seemed not to realize that her state of mind would not, could not change. "You wait until you get back home, Athena, you'll forget that fellow. After all, what can he bring you? He has no fortune and what do we know about him?"

No use to tell him that she did not care about his lack of fortune—did not suspect him of emulating Eames, as Ares had hinted. Nor did she find anything sinister in the mystery surrounding him. Knowing him as she did, she deemed it impossible that he could ever have done anything that was not honorable. She loved him, but Ares would not want to hear that. Even though he had admitted that the accusations he had hurled at Mr. Herriot on that dreadful day at the monastery were based on supposition rather than fact, even though he had apologized to him, he still disliked him.

Her brow contracted. In memory, she was back at the monastery again, seeing her brother come limping out. In her wild joy at knowing he was

162

alive, the marks on his face had failed to make any impression on her. Then, in shock, she heard him brand Mr. Herriot a coward who had left him to the mercies of a savage mob, which had felled and trampled him and might have killed him, had he not been rescued by a seaman from the *Apollo*. He had further accused his courier of having ravished his sister—this last supposition based on the seaman's tale of having seen Mr. Herriot bear Athena away.

She moaned. Shortly after her brother had joined her, Mr. Herriot had emerged from the courtyard, striding past them without a word. She had cried out to him only to be struck across the face by Ares and called a shameless wanton and a whore. It had been too much for her. Shocked, confused and weary from the long journey, she had become ill again. It was three days before she was well enough to see even her brother. She had not wanted to see him, but by that time he had been in a most chastened mood.

"I apologize, Athena," he had said. "That man Farnill told me the truth of it and I immediately went to see him."

"Where is he," she had whispered.

"He is staying in the home of his mistress," had been the words that had hit her like so many blows.

"His . . . mistress?"

"Eustacia Palomides," he had clarified, giving her a pitying look. "I expect this will not be welcome news, my dear, but it's a long-standing affair. Those who know Herriot here in Athens say he's been dancing attendance on the lady for the last five years. Since meeting her, he's not had an eye for any other female. I do not find it surprising. She's very beautiful—the figure of an Aphrodite and a face to match. It's obvious that they adore each other. Wish him joy of the wench, my love; you are well out of it."

She had remembered the name of Eustacia Palomides. He had mentioned it. "He . . . he told me about her," she had said. "He said she was a friend."

"And so she is," Ares had returned, "very friendly. She is forever caressing him and he can scarce keep his eyes off her." Ares had been sympathetic but relieved. "I am glad the man was so considerate of you, my dear. I told him I owed him a great debt and that I hoped he would go with us to Parnassus, but that I would not hold him to the letter of the bet any longer. That pleased him. He as much as told me he did not want to see either of us again and then he asked me to pay him for his services— and I did."

"He wanted to be paid," she had whispered.

"Of course." Ares had been surprised. "I told you that was part of our agreement. I admit that he was not very gracious, but I expect I was harsh myself before I knew the truth of the matter. He always was damned stiff-necked, you know. Furthermore, my love, you might think you are compromised—but it's not true. I got Herriot to promise he'll say nothing and Farnill has also agreed not to reveal what he knows. You'll be able to take your place in society as if nothing had happened."

But something *had* happened; and because of that she did not care about her place in society; she did not care about anything except Sable Herriot, but he did not want to see her. He had not even come to inquire after her, though Ares had told her he knew of her illness through Farnill. She could not understand it. Naturally, he had been wounded by Ares's accusations, but it seemed to her that he should have been able to understand her brother's confusion and worry. He had been badly hurt and conceived himself to be terribly disfigured. Though this was an exaggeration and though she had assured him that he was as handsome as ever and rather more interesting-looking than before, he had not believed her; clearly it would be some time before he became reconciled to his appearance. It would also be some time before his badly sprained ankle healed completely, and he was one who chafed at inactivity. Yet Mr. Herriot had failed to take any of these circumstances into account. Since he was a man who did not lack sensitivity, his failure to forgive Ares's insults must mean that he had not loved her enough—or, more likely, that he had not loved her at all. He had merely been doing his duty and he had been paid for that. Yet, if he had not loved her, he had been her friend. Would not a friend have made at least a token gesture of . . . friendship? Would he not have come at least once— he who had sat beside her bed for five nights? It was very strange, very hard to comprehend, or perhaps it was not—perhaps seeing the living Aphrodite who was named Eustacia Palomides once more had . . .

A lock of her hair caught by the breeze flew across her eyes—she pulled it away and touching her eyes, found them wet. She had not even known she was weeping—why weep over a man who did not want her, who preferred his mistress to her, who had not even tried to see her. Of course, she and Ares had spent a fortnight in Delphi . . . .

Delphi. She did not like to think of that time. They had traveled to Delphi in the company of Mr. Farnill and a competent guide. Yet, despite her love of her parents, despite the reason for the journey, she had not wanted to go. She had hated every moment of the long ride, envisioning Mr. Herriot at each turn of the road. His presence had seemed far more real to her than that of her brother or Mr. Farnill.

The brief, improvised ceremony of scattering their parents' ashes on the slopes of the great mountain had not, to her surprise, been dreadful or morbid. The clear, almost palpable light that bathed Parnassus and Delphi seemed to receive the strewn, fire-cleansed remnants of mortality with time-worn acceptance; and in a few moments the ashes of the senior Penroses were mingled with the soil of the land they had loved.

There was an atmosphere about Delphi that had amazed Athena. It seemed to her that those shattered rocks and deserted ruins lying under the mighty shadow of Parnassus were still part of a god-held sanctuary. Apollo . . . Pallas Athena . . . the place had been sacred to both and One had remained. She had felt the Presence.

In the early dawn of her second morning in Delphi, she had gone to a tiny shattered temple and prayed to that Presence, invoking its protection and its intercession; and in that moment she had actually thought herself invaded by the transcendant ecstasy that had moved the Pythonesses to speak with the tongue of the god. It was an experience that had remained with her; and, coming back to Athens, she had been positive that her prayer was answered and that, once back at their lodgings, she would hear that Sable had been to see her. However, in answer to her eager questions, the man Ares had left in charge had shaken his head, assuring her that no visitors had arrived in their absence. Her so-called ecstasy had been only a vain hope buoyed by imagination.

From the distance of a month, she could look back upon that time she had spent with Mr. Herriot as yet another period in which she had given free rein to that imagination. He had never really cared for her—he had only been fulfilling his agreement. No, no, no, she could not believe that. He had had some feeling for her—though not as much as she had believed—but she could not have been utterly mistaken. And that morning at the monastery when he had promised: "Soon"—surely, he must have meant *something* . . . But it did no good to speculate upon that. She lifted her hand to rub temples that had begun to throb again and heard a little metallic sound. Her reticule had bumped against the pillar, and inside it was the small, silver-mounted pistol that Ares had given her when they had gone to Delphi.

"For protection," he had said, his eyes somber.

"Protection . . ." she repeated to herself now. "If only I had the courage that Papa had—when Mama died . . . ."

A gust of laughter startled her. A quick glance over her shoulder showed her a pair of young men—English by the look of them—walking through the Parthenon. "And did she expect that he had intentions of coming back to her?" one asked.

Athena tensed. The question seemed almost directly applicable to her.

"She did, poor girl. She actually believed that she was his sole mistress. I imagine he always tries to give his conquests that impression—he loathes quarrels."

"Egad," the first man laughed, "it's a pity that

there was none to tell her that Byron has found himself a mistress on every island from Rhodes to the Shetlands."

"I expect she will know it before she's much older," his friend shrugged as they passed out of earshot.

Athena braced herself against the pillar. Ares had known Lord Byron at Cambridge. Just the other day, he had remarked that he was sorry to have missed "old George,"—Byron having been in Athens, leaving around the first of the year. Ares had praised his bent for poetry, this man who had more than one mistress. She swallowed painfully. On the way to the Acropolis that morning, Ares had tapped her arm and pointed to a house not far from the hill—distinctive because of two pillars, one on either side of its door. "That, my dear," he had said with a contemptuous little laugh, "is where your brother humbled himself."

"What can you mean?" she had inquired.

"I mean that it is—should we call it the temple or the bower of the beauteous Eustacia?—or perhaps I might dub her Aspasia—for she is known to keep a literary salon, though I'd not characterize Herriot as Pericles."

She had not answered him. She could not have spoken; her hurt was too deep for that. She had glanced at the house only once, but every feature of it was impressed on her mind, because *he* was there. He was there . . . and Byron had more than one mistress. Byron had had many mistresses, but Sable did not want her—he had not even come to see her, not in a whole month. And because of that she felt dead inside, and would continue to feel that way for the rest of her life. Her mind went back to that forsaken girl who had loved Byron. Had she known that she was one of many? Would she have cared? Byron was very beautiful, an exciting, brilliant, talented, wild young man. And who was it had said, "One crowded hour of glorious life is worth an age without a name?"

The quotation had applied to a war, but it was equally cogent here, and she was reasonably sure that whoever the girl was, she had been happy for at least a little while, because she had loved and been loved.... Love was often termed ephemeral, and one crowded hour, though it might not suffice for a lifetime, was better than nothing, nothing, *nothing* .... Perhaps if Sable were to see her again ... She knew that she could not leave Greece without seeing him. And if she were to see him and tell him ...

She glanced across the broken ground to the Porch of the Caryatids. Ares had said he was going there. If she were to leave from the front of the Parthenon, he would not be able to see her, not if she were careful. Determinedly, she went back, keeping close to the pillars; and finally she was at that mass of pillars and broken walls called the Propylaea that stood at the western entrance to the hill. Hastily, she made her way down the steps, and finally she was on the cactus-bordered path. The wails of the horde of starving cats that haunted the place were in her ears, but nothing else, no shout from above—Ares had not seen her leave. He would be worried, frantic, but she could not think of that; she could think only of the little house with the pillars.

The house had seemed only a short distance from the Acropolis, but that had been by carriage. On foot, it was further than she had realized. It took her full a half-hour to reach it, and by that time she was winded and her walking dress, a blue foulard, clung damply to her body; but for all that, she kept her cloak close about her and her hood down on her forehead as she dropped the door-knocker against its plate.

As she waited, a host of fears plagued her. Suppose no one was there—suppose he had gone away, suppose Madam Palomides would not admit her? It was taking an unconscionable long time to answer her knock and she ought not to be there. He would not want to see her—he had made that very clear—she must leave, go back to the Acropolis or home and give her brother some excuse about feeling faint. She must not be seen standing on the doorstep of the house that belonged to Sable's mistress. She . . .

A woman, short, plump, with black beady eyes, opened the door, looking at her interrogatively. Speaking in Greek, Athena said, "I wish to see Madam Palomides."

The woman, obviously a servant, eyed her dubiously. Athena could see she had many questions for and about this caller who came without invitation. Tears filled her eyes. "I must see her," she cried. "I must." The woman gave her a blank stare and she realized she had spoken in English. "I must see her," she repeated in Greek and, fearful lest the servant shut the door in her face, she pushed her way into the hall, ignoring the shrill, angry protests that followed her.

"But what is amiss, Xenia?" A small, dark woman came hurrying into the hall, coming to a dead stop and staring at Athena in amazement. She was, Athena guessed, probably Madame Palomides's housekeeper.

Before she could add her voice to that of the

angry maid, Athena cried, "I wish to see Madame Palomides. Please will you take me to her?"

The little woman said quietly, "I am Madame Palomides. What is it that you wish?"

"Mr. Herriot," Athena blurted and flushed. Clasping her hands, she continued, "Please, Madame, I must see him. He does not want to see me, but tomorrow I leave Athens and I . . . I must see him." Madam Palomides was suddenly framed in a nimbus of tears. Yet, even in the midst of her anguish, she was surprised. Contrary to what Ares had told her, Madame Palomides was no Aphrodite—she was not beautiful, she doubted that she ever had been beautiful. She did have lovely eyes, compassionate, understanding eyes—but she was well past her first youth. There were lines in her face and the figure, which had been so highly praised by her brother, was dumpy rather than lithe. Then, her impressions were scattered by the realization of her own temerity. What must this woman think of her impassioned outburst—she was staring at her in such a strange way, as well she might! "Oh, please, I am sorry, but . . . but . . ." She reached out her hands and, amazingly, Madam Palomides grasped them.

"You must be Athena Penrose," she said wonderingly.

"Yes, I—I am. I should have told you." She paused, adding tentatively, "I expect Mr. Herriot has . . . mentioned me."

"Come in here, my dear." With a dismissing look at the maid, Madam Palomides drew Athena into a small, simply furnished drawing room. Indicating a couch, she said, "Please sit down."

Because she felt as if her feet would no longer bear her, Athena obeyed. Her heart was pounding and she felt almost as if she was going to faint, but she would not crown her unforgivable display with that. She must endeavor to maintain what was left of her equilibrium. She took several deep breaths and felt a little better but still, she was horribly ashamed of herself. She had flouted all the rules of polite conduct. She had forced her way into this woman's house—this pleasant little lady who was the mistress of the man she loved. She did not know what to say. She sat there clasping and unclasping her hands and that was wrong, too. She had lost all sense of herself—she was behaving with an entire want of decorum. "Madame, I—I do not know what you must think . . ." she began.

"I do not know what I must think, myself." Madame Palomides gave her a searching look. "In these last weeks, I have hated you. I have thought you cruel and heartless for the way you have treated my poor Sable."

"For the way I have treated him?" Athena repeated. "But I have not seen him."

"That I know," Madame Palomides said. "Several times, he went to your house. Always he was turned away."

"Turned away?" Athena whispered.

"Your brother said you had no wish to see him. At first, he could not believe it, but finally your brother showed him a note you had written, a polite little note thanking him for his services and offering to recompense him for his care of you. When he came back . . " Madame Palomides shuddered. "I have not seen Sable in such a taking, ever. He does not eat, he does not sleep, he cannot write. I have told him again and again that one so cruel is not worth such pain." She paused and looked searchingly at Athena. "But I think that something is wrong— something is very wrong."

"Yes . . . something is very wrong. My brother lied to him and to me. He said Sable no longer wanted to see me. He said he was only . . . but that does not matter. Oh, Madame, where is he? I must tell him the truth, please. Is he here?"

"He is in the garden. I will let him know that you have come, but . . ." Madame Palomides looked at her dubiously. "But it is possible . . . he is now angry. His pride—he has much pride—he may tell himself he does not wish to see you."

"Then let me go to him, now," Athena begged. "I . . . I know that I ask a good deal of you since you love him, too, but please . . ."

"My poor child, I will not stand in your way, yet do not expect that he will be over-cordial. He has suffered much. But enough—come this way."

The garden lay at the back of the house. It was unexpectedly large and, though the year was well into autumn, numerous flowers still bloomed in patterned beds and the air was heady with the scent of jasmine blossoms. Pointing to a graveled path flanked on either side by high hedges, Madame Palomides said softly, "Go that way. You will find him sitting by a little pool. It is in the midst of a planting of cypresses."

Athena nodded. She had found she could no longer speak. Her heart seemed to have slipped its moorings and climbed to her throat. Thoughts and fragments of thoughts sped through her mind—many of them concerned her brother and his known dislike of Mr. Herriot. She should never have believed all he had told her. That she had showed a lack of faith in Sable, and perhaps even if she told him the truth he would blame her, but she could not think of that yet. She hurried down the path, and there were the cypress trees and the gleam of something white between them, just as there had been outside that village—and coming through those trees, she had discovered a temple and a broken pedestal and he had been there with her and now ... She had reached the trees.

She clutched at the rough, spiky greenery, steadying herself and swallowing air-bubbles of fear as she wondered if, after all, it would not have been better to let Madame Palomides prepare him for her coming—but then he might have refused to see her. His pride, his poor pride ...

Gritting her teeth, she slipped past the trees and saw the pool, round, clear and set in a wide marble basin. Mr. Herriot was sitting on a marble bench, staring into the water. His back was to her. She moved forward to stand behind him and as she did, she saw her reflection on the surface of the pool and knew he must see it, too, but if he did, he made no move and spoke no word, continuing to sit there, unmoving. That terrified her. She stepped closer to him.

"Sable," she managed to murmur.

He tensed. Rising, he slowly turned toward her. "I thought I had only imagined I saw your image," he said. His eyes hardened. "But why are you here, Miss Penrose?"

Her hopes had risen at his first words but now they were dashed by the coldness of his tone, the unfriendliness of his gaze. It was as impersonal as if he were looking at a stranger. He was so thin, so gaunt—there were dark hollows around his eyes. She longed to put her arms around him and draw him to her breast. But Madame Palomides was right; he had been hurt, terribly hurt and there was more than a chance that he would never forgive her. But he had asked her a question and he was waiting

174

for her answer. "I had to come. I had to see you before . . . We are leaving Athens tomorrow. We are returning to England, and . . . and . . ."

"*And* you thought it courteous to say your farewells in person, Miss Penrose. Why did you not write me a note as before—or have you come to press money upon me? I told your brother I would not accept it. Did he not convey you that message? I do thank you, though. It was a fair amount. You were very generous."

"That is not why I came, Sable," she said, pleased because her anguish did not cloud her voice. What she had to tell him must be clearly understood. She must not weep. She must be poised and dignified. "I came . . . because in the Acropolis this morning I heard two men talking about Byron." She hesitated, gathering her strength for the next statement, which, she knew must surprise him and, no doubt, shock him, but he must know the truth.

Before she could continue, he spoke, saying coldly, "People will always talk about Byron—he is a very romantic figure, but surely you did not come here to discuss Byron with me?" His tone was sarcastic but it seemed to her that she read uncertainty in his glance.

Athena lifted her chin, "One of the men said that B-Byron had several mistresses . . . ." She paused and again, to her chagrin he interrupted her.

"That is common gossip, Miss Penrose. And you wanted to share it with me. I must say I find that passing strange and—"

She flung out her arms. "Please!" she cried. "I—I wanted to t-tell you that if you could spare me a little c-corner of your life, I—I know you will say that I am completely lacking in pride, but pride

175

does not mean anything to me now, Sable. I do not know much about mistresses save that Ares has t-told me that Madame Palomides is your mistress and your great love ... and that is why you d-did not want me any more. But if ... if Byron can have several, maybe you could have t-two and I just want to be with you. I could be your second mistress, because you see—if I cannot be with you, cannot see you, cannot touch you, I ... I do not want to live any longer." She could no longer restrain her tears. All the pent-up agony of the past weeks was in them as, sinking down, she lay at his feet, her head buried in the grass.

"Athena ..." His voice was unsteady. Kneeling beside her, he drew her into his arms, stroking her hair, kissing her forehead and her cheeks as he had on a long-ago day in the mountains. Then it had been play-acting, but no longer. His kisses were not gentle. There was passion in them, passion in the way he held her so close against his heart, and passion in his voice as he said, "Athena, love, dearest, dearest love, look at me," and when she could finally raise her tear-strained face, there was even more passion in the long kiss he pressed upon her lips.

The carriage stopped before the house Athena shared with her brother on a quiet street near the British consulate in Athens. Standing just beyond the gates, Athena looked up into Mr. Herriot's concerned and angry eyes. "But I must see him alone. We decided that already, my dearest."

"I know, but I do not like it," he returned grimly.

"Love—" she reached up to caress his cheek— "you will only quarrel. I can see that you are primed for it. Then, one of you will issue a challenge which the other, out of honor, will not be able to refuse. I do not want my brother to shoot the man I love; I do not want the man I love to shoot my brother, not because of my feeling for him, but because of the memory of my parents whose only son he is. I promise I shall tell him of our agreement and come back quickly. Wait for me in the carriage, I beg you."

He still stared at her concernedly. "He might try to hold you . . ."

"I assure you that he will not."

"If you are not back shortly . . ."

"I give you leave to storm the barricades, but I pray you'll allow me a reasonable time before you resort to such measures." With a loving squeeze of his hand, she hurried toward the door.

In the few steps the journey took, she had a brief moment to wonder at the icy rage and determination that flooded her. Ares, her beloved brother and companion . . . Ares, whose supposed loss she had mourned so deeply . . . how came it that she was seeking, almost relishing, the confrontation which might well sever the bond between them for all time? Well, it had been his own acts that had brought this about. He had callously deceived her, deceived Sable, had played the part of an enemy to the man she loved. And that meant that, brother or no, Sir Ares Penrose had made an enemy of Athena Penrose—and one he might find even less to his liking than a troop of yataghan-wielding Turks!

A flurried servant admitted her and she came into the parlor to find Ares, cane in hand, limping back and forth across the floor, his expression one of the deepest anxiety. On seeing her, that anxiety changed swiftly to anger. "Where have you been?" he shouted.

177

She stared back at him contemptuously. "I paid a courtesy call, dear Ares."

He paled and the hand that clutched his cane turned yellow with tension. "You've been to see Herriot," he accused.

"Yes."

"And I expect he told you—"

"He told me nothing, but the woman, you called his 'great love ... the living Aphrodite' had much to say. However, I've not come here to discuss your duplicity."

"It was for your own good. Herriot's naught but an arrant fortune hunter."

"I would prefer you did not hurl such accusations at the man I am going to marry."

"As your guardian, I will not have it."

"You have accused my fiancé of wanting to marry me for my fortune. It is not a particularly flattering conclusion—" she began coldly.

"He is not your fiancé. I tell you I will not allow it. And you are besotted if you think he wants you for any other reason. On the ship—"

"Much has happened since then."

"And what does that much entail? Can it be that after all you have not been frank with me? Can it be that you find yourself having no other choice but to wed him?"

"I am not going to bear his child, if that is what you are so delicately hinting, Ares. I pray you'll stop arguing with me. However, in view of your beliefs, it will no doubt please you that at the request of my fiancé, I am deeding my part of the estate to you— because contrary to your cherished beliefs, Mr. Herriot will not marry me unless I agree to come to him with nothing save myself."

"The man is mad!"

"Be that as it may, those are his terms." Reaching into her reticule, she brought forth a paper. "This is the agreement, leaving you my part of the estate—it is quite legal, signed by me and witnessed by Madame Palomides and her servant." She thrust the paper at him.

His face was white with anger and his scar glowed like a brand upon it. "You are being duped in some way of which you have no notion. However, it does not matter. As your guardian I have final say—and I say that if he continues to pursue you, I shall call him out and—"

"I expected that you would say that. Mr. Herriot is a good shot and I imagine he is also an excellent swordsman. However, you will *not* call him out, you will *not* continue to assert your so-called guardianship, nor will you make trouble of any kind. Instead, you will give me your sworn word that you will not interfere in any way—for if you refuse—"

"I do refuse," he barked.

"If you refuse," she continued, reaching into her reticule again and bringing out her small pistol, "I shall shoot you in the shoulder and devil take the consequences!"

He paled. "You would not!"

She cocked the pistol. "I would."

He backed off, staring at her uncertainly. "You . . ."

"Swear by your honor. No, do not swear by your honor—I have ceased to believe in that. Swear by almighty God and by the souls of our parents."

"You could not shoot me, Athena," Ares cried. "You could not."

"You are wrong, my brother. I could do it quite easily, especially when I think of your knavery

179

where Mr. Herriot is concerned and of the tortures you have inflicted upon me these past weeks and which I might have been forced to endure for the rest of my life! You, who knew of his kindness to me and . . . but no matter. I am going to count to three." She held the pistol steadily, aiming at his right shoulder. "One . . . two . . ."

"I swear!" he choked.

"By almighty God and by the souls of our parents?"

"Yes, yes."

"Say it."

"I . . . swear by almighty God and by the souls of our parents . . ."

"That you will leave us in peace."

"That I will leave you in peace."

"That was wise," she said coldly. Slipping her gun back into her reticule, she added, "I will bid you farewell, Ares."

"Athena," he took a step toward her, "I did it for your own good, that I swear also, because I love you." He blinked and she saw that there were tears in his eyes. "Will I never see you more?"

She had thought her heart wholly hardened against him, but she had been mistaken. His villainy had not destroyed all that she had felt for him throughout her life. She said, "If my husband agrees to it, we will meet, but not soon, Ares . . . not soon." She went on out, closing the door softly behind her.

Eleven

It was early morning, but Athena, hearing a noise in the room, awakened immediately and sat up to find her husband standing at the window. Beyond him, the inn yard was white.

"Oh," she murmured, "it snowed during the night."

He turned immediately and came back to her, sitting down on the edge of the wide four-poster bed. Folding her in his arms, he kissed her passionately. She clung to him. Though they had been married all of two months, waking to his embrace was still as exciting as it had been on their wedding voyage back to England. Yet this morning she felt a certain tenseness about him. Gently pushing a tendril of hair out of his eyes, she said concernedly, "What is troubling you, my dearest?"

He cocked a quizzical eye at her. "Why should you think that I am troubled, my beautiful?"

"Because I know you."

He did not answer at once and she realized that throughout this journey, he had been edgy. She wondered at that. They had been invited to spend the Yuletide season at the home of his publisher, the son of a prosperous coal-miner who had built him-

181

self a fine estate in an obscure corner of Northumberland. Sable had told her about the invitation rather reluctantly, saying apologetically that he knew she might not be used to moving in such circles, yet the man in question, though a "cit," was well-bred and a gentleman. She had told him gently that she did not think of circles, only of numbers that equaled two, but he had returned diffidently, "Shall you mind giving up . . ."

Knowing what he had been about to say, she had slipped her hand over his mouth, telling him, "I will never mind anything. I should not mind living in a cottage such as we shared in Greece if I could wake and find your arms around me." He had seemed satisfied with that answer—but this morning his doubts appeared to have returned in full measure. "What is troubling you, Sable, love?" she repeated.

He gave her a nervous smile. "Shall we say that I am about to embark upon something I have never attempted before . . ."

"What would that be?"

"A . . . novel."

"Oh!" Her relief found expression in a merry laugh.

"Do you find that so amusing?" he asked with a touch of hauteur.

"No, I am only pleased that it is not something more weighty. You cannot be troubled by that, surely."

"Can I not? I have never attempted to write a novel."

"I have every faith that it will be as fine a work as your other beautiful books, my dear."

He embraced her again. "You cannot judge until you have heard the plot. Should you like me to give it to you now?"

"Oh, yes."

"You are not too sleepy?"

"Not at all, but I am a little chilly." Her laughing eyes held an invitation he did not resist. Slipping beneath the covers, he pulled her into his arms.

Some time later, Athena said softly, "You promised to tell me the plot of your novel."

His eyes lingered lovingly on her face. "Perhaps it's slipped my memory."

"Oh, no," she protested. "I hope not."

"Well, as it happens, your hopes can be realized. I am quite anxious to see if you will approve it."

"I know I shall," she murmured.

His tenseness had returned. "You may not—but no matter, this is the way of it. It begins in the home of Lord Atherstone, a nobleman of mature years—say fifty. He is married to a beautiful young wife. She is not his first wife. The first Lady Atherstone, who was also beautiful, had borne him one child, a son. The boy, whom we will call Arthur, was thirteen when his mother was killed in a hunting accident. It was a great shock to him for he and his mother were very close. However, he was equally fond of his father, and, in time, he recovered from his grief, though he still missed his mother greatly.

"Then Lord Atherstone was invited to the house of a friend for the grouse-shooting season. There he met a widow named Lady Hammond; she had her daughter with her, a beautiful girl of nineteen. Though the widow exerted her wiles to charm him, it was the daughter who won his heart. Rosalie was her name, and she seemed to love him. Lady

183

Hammond was understandably annoyed; she protested that there was too great a disparity in their ages, but finally she was won over and Rosalie Hammond became the Countess of Gore, which was the family name.

"Arthur, who had turned sixteen, was exceedingly surprised by his father's choice of a wife. Of course, no one, in his estimation, was worthy to replace his mother in his father's affections, but still he had to agree that Rosalie was very beautiful; and on the few occasions that he saw her with his father, she seemed to be truly loving. Still, it was difficult for him to welcome a stepmother who was but three years his senior. He wished, in fact, that he were not being tutored at home—he was due to enter Oxford University at eighteen, but meanwhile he remained at the castle. Though he tried to avoid the second Lady Atherstone as much as possible, she—"

"Why did he do that?" Athena cut in.

"Oh, did I not tell you?" Sable smiled mirthlessly. "She was forever following him about—or at least it seemed that way to him. If he went riding, she would either join him at the stables or meet him in the park. If he went to work in his library, she would come in to take a book, asking him prettily what he would recommend. His father, you see, was away a great deal of the time. He had vast estates and, being a very responsible man, he did not depend on his stewards alone to keep them in order and see to the demands of his tenants. Rosalie was restless in his absence. She did not like living so far from London. She told Arthur that there was nothing for her to do, nowhere to show off the beautiful gowns and jewels her husband had lavished upon her. Reminded that there were balls given on neighboring estates, she complained that these did not take place often enough to suit her. She talked wistfully of Almacks and Vauxhall and the opera. Since his father had begged him to be pleasant to his wife, Arthur could not avoid her, but he did not like her and furthermore, as time went on, he began to notice a certain coolness between himself and his father, which he did not understand.

"Then, one night, Arthur awakened from a deep sleep to find Rosalie in his room, her hair unbound and wearing a very revealing nightdress. He was surprised and shocked. 'What are you doing in here?' he demanded. 'Is something wrong?'

"'Oh, yes, very wrong, Arthur, dearest, very, very wrong,' she wept. 'I am so lonely and your Papa is away so much of the time and . . .' She sat down on the edge of his bed and put her arms around his neck. 'Be kind to me, Arthur,' she murmured. 'Please be kind to me . . .' And then she kissed him, and that is how his father found them."

"Oh, how . . . how dreadful!" Athena exclaimed.

"Yes, it was, rather. I should think, however, that it will make a good scene in my novel."

She had forgotten that he was giving her the plot of a novel. It had seemed very real. "Oh, yes, it should. But what happened, then, to poor Arthur?"

"Well, it seemed very damning for poor Arthur, especially since Rosalie began to cry and sob and say that he had forcibly dragged her into his room and had his way with her."

"But his father would not believe that?"

"Would he not? Well, the father that I have . . . conceived, did. You see he had been warned by one among the servants who had seen Arthur and Rosalie together. That is why he had come back unexpectedly. Furthermore, he preferred to give his wife

185

the benefit of any doubts he might have entertained. She was, as I said, very beautiful. Arthur, branded a rogue and a ravisher, left that night. He had a hard time of it—he took no money with him.

"When I write the book, I shall enlarge upon all that befell him after his departure, but suffice to say that it was a difficult period. Then, Arthur found he had a talent for . . . painting. He began in a small way, but his work came to the attention of a well-known artist, who, perceiving that he had promise, took him into his studio. In a year or so, he began to get commissions and at length, he became a successful portrait painter. Word of his success reached his father, who immediately wrote to him, telling him that he had been searching for him and that his stepmother had crowned numerous follies by eloping with an under-footman. He told his son that he knew the truth and begged him to come home, but Arthur coldly refused."

"Oh, why?" Athena demanded.

"Because his pride was grievously wounded— his father had taken his stepmother's word against his. Arthur could not forgive him for that."

"Oh, the poor father," she murmured.

"You do not feel sorry for Arthur, I see?"

"I do, but his father must have been very lonely, deprived of his son; and he must truly have repented. It might be that he was proud, too. I believe Arthur ought to have taken that into account—but I expect I should not say that."

His arm tighened about her. "Why should you not say it?"

"Because it is your book and you know how you wish to portray your characters. What happened to Arthur?"

"The story is not yet completed."

"Oh," she said disappointedly, "I should like to know the rest."

He lifted a strand of her hair to his lips and kissed it. "I promise that you shall when I have decided upon the ending."

"I hope that will be soon."

"I am pleased that my plot has held your interest. I shall confide it to my publisher, when we arrive at his estate. I hope it will be worth a reasonable advance."

She bit back a little sigh. It occurred to her that Sable might have been writing about himself, when it came to pride. If he had only accepted her large dowry, he would not need to worry about advances.

"You are looking pensive, my love," he remarked. "If I had a pura, I shold offer it to you for your thoughts."

Her eyes shone at the reference. "And I should tell you, as I told you then, that they are worth nothing."

"Athena, love, wake up."

Startled, Athena lifted her head from her husband's shoulder and glanced out of the window of their hired post-chaise. She saw they had come out of the forest which, he had told her, bordered his publisher's estate and were now at the end of a long driveway. "Oh, have we arrived?" she asked.

"We are nearly there."

Looking out of the window, she saw a wide expanse of snow-covered ground planted with tall trees, their bare branches gleaming with icicles. In the distance rose a massive building centered by a great turreted tower. "But it is a castle!" she exclaimed.

"Yes. Before he bought it, the estate was in the

family of the Marquis of Ainsworth—but the last heir died."

"Oh, it is lovely," she breathed.

"Lovely?" he questioned with a slight smile. "I should say stately or dignified, but I do not know if I would call it lovely."

"I would," she insisted, "because I do love castles."

"Do you?" He gave her a quizzical look.

"Yes, but I should not like to live in one," she assured him hastily.

"Why not?"

"Oh, they are so grand. And . . ."

"And you are thinking I could not afford such grandeur and you are striving to spare my feelings," he finished.

She blushed. "Nothing of the sort. Such a thought never occurred to me."

"Did it not?" He kissed her cheek.

"I assure you, Sable . . ."

"Shhh, we've not the time for an argument. We are at the door."

He was tense again, very tense. Seeing his set face, Athena was disturbed. No doubt he was worried about the reception his publisher would give that projected novel. Yet, looking at him, she felt a little thrill of pride. He was so handsome, so distinguished. It was hard indeed to remember him as the weary, ragged man she had known in Greece. Though he had no valet to dress him and though his clothes were not new, no one would have guessed it. His coat was of good cloth, a dark gray that complemented his eyes. His tight-fitting buckskin breeches showed off his admirable figure and no valet could have fashioned a more intricately-tied cravat or imparted a higher gloss to his Hessian boots. His dark hair was fashionably coiffed; she frowned at the threads of white, more noticeable now. She attributed many of them to the painful month in Athens when Ares . . . But now was no time to think of that period, for the Furies would be rising again.

Glancing down, she saw her wide sable muff, a wedding gift from a bemused Aunt Caroline; it matched the sable trim on her blue coat. That and her gown, a Parisian import, again in her favorite blue, had been purchased the previous winter and must do for many winters to come—then the sable could be removed and used for another coat. She smiled. Amazing that the rich Miss Penrose must think of such shifts—she would need to learn sewing and ironing. There was a chance that in lean times she would need to iron her husband's shirts. The prospect did not daunt her. She had already learned to exist without an abigail. Her hair looked almost as well as when Jane had had the care of it. She was glad of that; she wanted to appear at her best. His publisher would no doubt be curious about his author's bride. She ran her hand down his arm and found it rigid.

"Love, do not fret," she whispered. "He cannot but approve the tale—it is really most compelling."

Before he could respond, the chaise had come to a stop and a footman had opened the door and set the steps down for them.

The entrance hall of the castle was very large. Evidently, the present owners had done nothing to alter the original workmanship. It was paneled in rich old wood and extending from an upper gallery, heavy with carving, were flags emblazoned with coats of arms which she guessed must have been newly invented by the publisher. There was a huge fireplace topped by a sculptured stone mantel; over

189

it hung an ancient shield, bearing the same crest as had appeared on the flags—it looked authentic, but such effects were easy to achieve. In one corner, she saw a suit of armor and smiled—when inventing ancestors, it was best to go all the way, she supposed. However, the whole was really beautiful and more tasteful than she had anticipated. Furthermore, she did not think that Sable need worry about his publisher's reception. Obviously, he was an honored guest; the butler had looked upon him with real affection.

"Will it be a large house party?" she asked.

"I do not believe so," he answered absentmindedly; his tenseness had increased. Then, she heard footsteps and, looking toward an archway, saw a man framed in it. He stood there for a moment, a little uncertainly, she thought. Then he came forward. He was in his mid-sixties, conservatively dressed and more distinguished in appearance than she had expected. There was something oddly familiar about him. This puzzled her, for she knew she had never met him. Coming to a stop, a few feet away from them, he stared fixedly at Sable.

To her surprise, her husband looked back at him in much the same manner—then made a tentative step forward. "Father," he said, and held out his hand.

"My dear boy!" There was a suspicious brightness in the eyes of the older man as he strode forward to grasp Sable's hand. He held it warmly in both of his. "My dear, dear boy, welcome home."

Sitting in what her father-in-law, the far-from-defunct Marquis of Ainsworth, was pleased to call "the small drawing room," an immense tapestried chamber with high, carved ceilings and filled with

190

furniture that had been brought from a French chateau as part of the dowry of Alys de Ventadour, who had married Sable's great-grandfather, the Sixth Marquis, Athena looked dazedly at the man whose full name, she now knew to be Frederick Arthur Justin Sable Herriot-Crozier.

It all seemed like a dream from which she half expected to be awakened. However, no dream could have contained so many varied and vivid images: the magnificent dining room with its long polished table at which a Herriot-Crozier had entertained his Majesty Charles II, who had presented him with the immense silver épergne that stood in the center of that same table. She had been taken into other rooms, the beautiful long gallery with its portraits of Herriot-Croziers back to the time of Henry II; there had been a lovely old chapel and a beautiful old library; everything had been beautiful or magnificent or lovely and old, but at present her mind could encompass none of it, not even the fact that rather than being plain Mrs. Herriot, she was Lady Herriot-Crozier.

Her Lord looked at her adoringly, then turning to the Marquis, broke a short companionable silence by saying, "You know, Father, we owe a great debt to my wife."

The Marquis smiled at Athena and, seeing that smile, she wondered why she had not guessed at the relationship between father and son immediately. He said, "I am already greatly indebted to her. It is a long time since a son of this house has brought home so beautiful a bride—and she has more than beauty, she has character."

"Yes," her husband said softly, "she does have character—and she taught me a most important lesson."

"Indeed?" the Marquis looked at him earnestly, "and what was that?"

"She has taught me the folly of pride."

"Ah," his father said, "then I am greatly in your debt, my dear." He rose and came forward to kiss her hand.

The bed on which Athena and her husband lay stood in the midst of the Gold Chamber, so called because of a gilded ceiling carved with fantastic flowers and because of gold-brocaded walls; the floral design was repeated in a magnificent gold and ivory damask canopy and on the quilted spread, now turned back for the night. In a large stone fireplace, leaping flames provided the only light in the room.

Lord Herriot-Crozier, lying close to his wife, said, "I could not tell you until I was entirely sure that I would be able to bridge the barrier between us. But you had already showed me the way, when you came to me that morning at Eustacia's house— what you said about pride stood me in good stead."

"I am glad. He loves you very dearly and I think you love him as much."

"Yes," he admitted a little throatily. He added quickly, "Then you approve the conclusion of my novel?"

She twined her arms around his neck. "Dearest, I am sure you know me well enough by now to understand that as an indefatigable reader of romances, I adore a happy ending!"